Sheila Tyrer Hughes's passion for reading developed naturally into a love of writing. After leaving school at seventeen, she worked as a trainee pathology lab technician before going to California in search of an adventure. There, she took care of children and horses before returning to Wales and becoming an English teacher. She loves mysteries, the countryside, ancient buildings and landscapes and losing herself in imaginary worlds. She is a mother and grandmother and lives in Cheshire. *The Mouse in the Teapot* is her third book for children.

The Mouse in the
Teapot

Sheila Tyrer Hughes

Illustrations by Bee Buckmaster

AUSTIN MACAULEY PUBLISHERS™
LONDON • CAMBRIDGE • NEW YORK • SHARJAH

A CIP catalogue record for this title is available from the British Library.

ISBN 9781528978743 (Paperback)
ISBN 9781528978750 (Hardback)
ISBN 9781528978774 (ePub e-book)

www.austinmacauley.com

First Published 2021
Austin Macauley Publishers Ltd®
1 Canada Square, Canary Wharf
London, E14 5AA
+44 (0)20 7038 8212
+44 (0)20 3515 0352

To the memory of Nan, my cousin and friend, who firmly believed my stories would one day find their way into beautifully illustrated books.

(Did you know that when a butterfly flutters its wings in Japan a ripple, be it ever so tiny, is felt around the world? As a result, the last leaf might fall from a tree in Little Sodbury, or a shower damp the dust in Lamington Lane.

So it is with everything. So it was with Charlie Pringle and Arthur's teapot. But instead of a butterfly disturbing the air, it was a sneeze. If a tiny butterfly can make a difference, just think what devastating consequences a sneeze can have.)

Charlie Pringle was like every other boy and girl I know. He had a dream. It wasn't an enormous, mind-boggling dream like watching giant manta rays from a submarine or journeying to the Moon or Mars. But it might as well have been.

All Charlie wanted was to own a mountain bike, even though there were no mountains in his part of town. He wanted to cycle through a forest with the wind in his face – to fly down mountain paths and bump over stones while buzzards circled overhead. He wanted to cool his face in water that gurgled up from the ground.

"Some hope," said Dad. "They cost a lot of money, they do."

"No chance," said Mum. "Sorry Charlie, but you need some new shoes for school. And anyway, what use would a bike be here? I'd never let you out on these streets. It's far too dangerous."

Stephen Cropper was having a bike for Christmas – and a real leather football – and a basketball net to hang on the garage door. He'd already got a computer and a TV and a music centre in his room.

Charlie Pringle hadn't even got a garage door. Stephen Cropper lived in a house with a garage and a garden with trees and a big, square lawn.

Charlie Pringle lived in a flat on the fourth floor, with windows overlooking the canal and a derelict shoe factory. The flats were called Priory Gardens, which seemed daft when there was only a tiny patch of grass and one sad-looking tree.

Charlie had no garden to play in, but that was OK. He'd never lived in a house with a garden so how could he miss it?

Sometimes Charlie would stare at the still, dark water of the canal and the empty shell of the factory with its boarded-up windows and faded signs. He liked to imagine the heavy horses with their heads down, plodding along the towpath, pulling barges loaded with coal. He tried to picture the bustle and heave of people leaving the factory when the whistle blew. There'd be lads working there who weren't much older than he was. He could almost see them when he looked out through the window. He had a wonderful imagination, had Charlie.

"I wonder what they had for Christmas," he would say to himself. "I don't suppose they could afford bikes either."

"You need a new mattress," said Mum.

Charlie didn't speak.

"Would you like a new football shirt?" she asked hopefully. It was cheaper than a bike – and Charlie liked playing football

Charlie tried to smile.

He wanted a mountain bike, and mountains to ride down. You couldn't have dreams about school shoes and mattresses. It wasn't the same.

"I'll earn some money," said Charlie one day as he watched two ducks paddling lazily down the canal. "Then I can help pay for it."

He didn't tell Stephen Cropper of course. Stephen Cropper's dad had a big new car. Charlie's dad had a bad back and an old Ford Fiesta. He worked as a caretaker at the local comprehensive.

Charlie didn't know who lived in most of the flats. Some of the flats were empty. He knew old Mrs Tyrer on the ground floor. She was the one who always shook her fist when the boys played football on the tiny square of grass by her window.

They weren't supposed to of course, but that was part of the fun.

Perhaps he could clean windows – indoors, of course, or go to the shops, or make someone a cup of tea. He was good at tea, was Charlie. He'd had plenty of practice when Mum was ill. That was after Mary-Lou had been born.

Well, in for a penny, in for a pound, as his granddad would say. He would start with Mrs Tyrer. It could only get easier after that.

Knock! Knock!

No answer.

Knock again.

This time a twitch of net curtain.

"Go away!"

Charlie fidgeted. Then he lifted the letterbox flap and shouted. "Do you want any jobs doing?"

"You a boy scout?"

"No. I'm Charlie Pringle. I live at Number Twenty-Six."

Silence. Charlie almost turned around and walked away. Then she said, "What can you do, Charlie Pringle?"

Charlie realised it was the first time he had heard her voice. It was remarkably strong for so old a lady.

He lifted his shoulders. He wasn't very big for ten. "Anything, Mrs Tyrer. Just try me."

Silence again. Charlie shrugged and turned to go. Then a chain rattled and the door opened – a little – not enough for a scrawny cat to get through.

"I know you, don't I?"

He nodded sheepishly.

"You on your own?"

He nodded again.

"Better come in, then. You can help me get Arthur's teapot down. I can't reach it anymore and I haven't washed it for years."

That's not going to earn me much, thought Charlie. *Still, it's a start.*

He followed the old lady down a short hall into the tiny living room. It smelled strange to Charlie, old like something out of a museum, or Madame Tussauds. It made him think of the war. He'd seen programmes on the TV, where the rooms are filled with heavy brown furniture and old radios, and there's weird stuff called linoleum on the floor. No one was allowed any chocolate, and women wore pinnies all the time and had strange hairdos. Mrs Tyrer's flat was just like that – as if she'd peeled the inside out of another, much older house and stuck it into this one.

"It's nice here," he said.

She looked sharply at him as if she didn't believe him. "What do you mean nice?"

"This place, the way you've done it. It's different from ours, the colours and that, and the furniture."

"Old-fashioned you mean?"

Charlie shrugged and smiled sheepishly.

She pointed to a wooden chair. It was old with a wobbly back and there was a flat cushion on its seat.

"There, you can stand on that. There's the teapot."

She pointed to the top of a china cabinet that stood on top of a chest of drawers and Charlie wondered if he could reach it even from a chair.

"Why do you keep it up there?" he asked.

"I've always kept it up there, safe from idle hands," she said.

Charlie put the chair in place and removed the cushion. Then he bent down to unfasten his trainers.

"Leave them on. They'll do no harm. And you might slip in your socks."

He climbed up. Through the glass doors of the cabinet, he saw faces smiling at him from old picture frames. He hesitated and couldn't help smiling back, especially at the girl in the nurse's uniform, sitting with some wounded soldiers. She reminded him of his Auntie Trish.

"What are you looking at?" Mrs Tyrer's voice was sharp as gravel, suddenly unfriendly and suspicious. "There's no money there, if that's what you're after!"

He felt as though he'd been punched in the stomach for no reason at all.

"I was just looking at the photos," he said.

He reached up, but couldn't quite get hold of the teapot. Another inch. He leaned forward a little further and just managed to hook the teapot handle with his finger. Mrs Tyrer had been holding the chair, but then she sneezed and the chair skidded on the linoleum floor. Charlie and Arthur's teapot crashed down together. Charlie had a soft landing on a horsehair sofa but the teapot was not so lucky. It landed on the lino and smashed into at least ten pieces.

"I'm sorry. The chair slipped. I couldn't help it."

Mrs Tyrer was blowing her nose, peering at him over the top of a large white handkerchief. She turned away and took hold of a long-handled broom that stood in a corner. He couldn't see her face. Was she mad at him? Was she going to wallop him with her broomstick? He didn't wait to find out, but jumped up from the sofa and fled, almost crashing into a sideboard as he escaped through the door.

That evening, Charlie was kneeling on his chair by the window, looking out across the canal. He often did that when he had something on his mind and wanted to think. It was as if this corner of the town and this view across the canal to the old factory belonged only to him. No one else's view would be exactly the same.

Tonight, there were two moons, one like a great silver ship in the sky and the other, a silk-sailed shallop gliding down the canal. It was a brilliant word, 'shallop'. He'd read it in a poem when they'd been studying King Arthur. Shallops had flitted silken-sailed down the river to Camelot. If only the canal would take Charlie to Camelot, a place full of heroes where there were brave knights and gleaming horses in jewelled bridles.

There were no stars that he could see. That was because of all the lights in the town. Their sickly yellow glow washed out the stars. Charlie wondered what the sky would look like from the top of a mountain where there was no smoky haze from street lamps. Moonlight was strange, he decided. Colours disappeared, but you could still see things. And the moon could throw shadows that were darker than the night. There was one now. A shadow with a life of its own – or something blowing across the factory yard. It was hard to make it out, but it was drifting towards the gate. Then it changed direction and moved around in a circle. It didn't look like a bin liner, and if you used your imagination a little, you could almost believe it was someone bent over shuffling about – looking for something, perhaps.

Then it headed for the gate again. Whatever it was, it would stop when it hit the gate and if it was a big bag, it would probably be caught there. He would see it in the morning, blowing like a flag.

Charlie screwed up his eyes, blinking in an effort to see more clearly. Then a cloud slid across the moon as if it was deliberately blotting it out. When Charlie looked again, the shadow was gone. There was nothing flapping on the gate and nothing blowing about in the yard. It puzzled him.

All weekend, Charlie kept well away from Mrs Tyrer's flat and didn't play football with the other boys. He tried not to think about what had happened, but it was hard. He knew it hadn't really been his fault, but he still felt guilty and silly. He shouldn't have run away like that. And the trouble was – it had put him off going anywhere else to look for jobs. Now he would never have a bike.

****

In school on Monday, Charlie's class began a new project about World War Two and they carried on with it all week. Mrs Taylor told them it was sixty years since the Blitz. "That's short for Blitzkrieg," she explained. "It means 'lightning attack' and that's exactly what it was."

She brought in a box containing an old gas mask and told them about children who were sent away from their homes and families in the cities. They went to live in the country with strangers and left everything they knew, behind. They'd worn labels to say who they were because some of them were not much bigger than Mary-Lou, and each one carried a gas mask in a box in case the Germans tried to poison them with gas-filled bombs.

She showed them pictures of children waiting in lines and standing in a station looking scared. They all had bare legs, even though it was winter – and the boys had short trousers and caps. Then she showed them black and white pictures of children on farms, wearing big Wellington boots and old jumpers. They were feeding chickens and ducks. Some of them looked happy and some of them didn't.

"Were you evacuated, Miss?" Amy Fellows asked, with that smile she always had when she was trying to be a goody-goody.

"Good heavens, no!" said Mrs Taylor.

"Weren't you born in the olden days?"

Charlie had looked at her in disgust. Girls were useless. They didn't know anything. Except Mary-Lou of course. She wouldn't be so daft.

She had him for a brother.

"The war was sixty years ago, wasn't it, Miss?" he said. "Don't you listen, Fellows?"

"Thank you, Charlie."

"And Mrs Taylor's only twenty-one, aren't you Miss?" He grinned. It's what his mum always said when anyone asked her how old *she* was.

"Thank you again, Charlie. But that's what I want you to think about. Your mums and dads are too young, but what about grandparents and great-grandparents. What do they remember about the war? Perhaps they were evacuated. Perhaps they were soldiers or nurses or land-army girls. I want you to ask them – like reporters, and I want you to write down at least one interesting story they remember about the war. And if they've got any photographs – that would be brilliant – or things like gas masks and ration books – or medals even. It would be lovely to see some medals and to hear about some real live heroes. Perhaps you could find people to come in and talk to us.

We'll make a big wall-frieze and your families can come and see it."

Of course, that got Charlie thinking again – about the pretty nurse with the cross on her white pinny who had smiled at him from Mrs Tyrer's china cabinet. And for some strange reason, it also set him thinking about the moon sailing down the canal and the shadow in the yard.

"Mum, was Nana in the war?"

"Fighting, you mean?"

"No! Don't be daft! Was she evacuated or anything? Can she tell me any stories about it?"

"I doubt it, love. She was only four when the war ended and they didn't live in a town."

"What about Granddad?"

"I don't think he remembers much about it either."

"Have I got any great-grandparents?"

"Not a one, I'm sorry."

15

Back to Mrs Tyrer. Charlie just couldn't get away from it because he couldn't stop thinking about her – and now there was this homework, and he just knew she would be able to help him. He hadn't told anyone about what had happened, especially not Stephen Cropper. So he told Mary-Lou; she was only eighteen months old and couldn't tell anyone.

"What shall I do, Loulou?" he said as she thumped some blocks with a plastic hammer.

"Googoo," said Mary-Lou helpfully.

"Hm! Is that what you think?" said Charlie, passing her yellow fluffy duck whose name was Googoo.

"Googoo," said his little sister again as she hit the duck with the plastic hammer.

"Glue?" said Charlie. "That's what you're saying. Good idea, though I'm not sure if it'll work. P'raps she's put Arthur's teapot in the bin already."

"Googoo," said Mary-Lou as if she thought it was a brilliant idea.

"OK," said Charlie, "but I bet I'll have to buy some special stuff. Can you lend me some money?"

Mary-Lou hit his foot with her hammer.

"It was a joke!" said Charlie.

In his room, Charlie emptied his moneybox onto the bed. Three pounds and seventy-two pence. He was supposed to be saving money – making it, not spending it. He sighed. He hadn't made a very good start, had he?

On Saturday morning, he went to the hardware store where he had to ask for help in choosing just the right glue. It was two tubes that you had to mix together and it took almost all of his money.

16

There were butterflies in his stomach when he knocked on Mrs Tyrer's door. He waited and waited. Just like before, it opened an inch and the old lady said, "Who is it? What do you want?"

"It's Charlie Pringle. I've brought some glue."

She didn't open the door any further.

"Glue? What for?"

"Arthur's teapot. You haven't thrown it in the bin, have you?"

"Of course I haven't. Why did you run off like that? Gave me quite a turn."

"I know. I'm sorry I ran away. I thought you were going to wallop me with the brush."

Then Charlie heard the strangest noise.

Mrs Tyrer was laughing, giggling just like Michelle Potts did when she had to sit by a boy. It made her sound much younger. Then the chain rattled and she pulled open the door.

"So you thought I was an old witch about to beat you with my broomstick, is that it?" And she laughed again. "I'm sorry if I scared you. It's my back," she said as she led the way into the living room, "and my knees. Can't bend down, you see. But I can use a long-handled brush." And she laughed again. "Wasn't your fault. Sneezes always come at the wrong time. I remember sneezing once when I was sucking a mint imperial or something. Lost it, I did, and didn't know where it had gone. I was talking to some soldiers at the time – not General Eisenhower," she looked slyly at him, "that was another day in Berlin, when that great bumble bee landed on me. – No, this was in Oxford, after Dunkirk.

They were a bonny bunch of lads. Always so cheerful, even when they couldn't walk. Then they started to laugh. 'Sorry, Nurse Hughes,' one of them said, 'but you've got a mint imperial stuck to your chin.' Face like a beetroot I had, and me trying to impress them with my cool efficiency."

She turned to look at him. "So you've brought some glue."

Charlie saw the teapot bits all laid out on a tray on the table. It was just as if she had been waiting for him to come and mend it. There was something else, too, something carved out of wood. Charlie picked it up. It was about six centimetres long and crudely cut, but he could see it was a mouse with tiny ears and a long tail curled around it. He liked it.

"Talking of mint imperials," said Mrs Tyrer, "it reminds me of that time in church, only that was a cough, not a sneeze … Still, you don't want to hear all that now, do you? Eeh, but it made us laugh, the way it bounced along the pews – and such a clatter when it finally fell to the floor. The vicar stopped speaking and then started telling us all about the Civil War and how the Roundheads had attacked the very church we were sitting in. There were shot marks in the door, he said. And if we didn't believe him, we could go and look. Of course we believed him, he was the vicar, wasn't he? But we still went to check up afterwards. Funny how one thing leads to another. Mint imperials one minute, Roundhead bullets the next."

This is promising, thought Charlie. *She obviously likes telling stories.*

They sat down at the table while Charlie pieced together the teapot. It was like doing a jigsaw puzzle. When he saw that the bits all fitted and nothing was missing, he read the instructions on the glue, mixed the glue on a jam pot lid and set to work.

****

Mrs Tyrer watched him, a frown on her face.

"I suppose you think I'm daft, keeping an old thing like that."

"Was it worth much?"

"Money, you mean. No, I shouldn't think so."

"Who's Arthur?"

"My husband."

"Is he dead?"

"Fifteen years ago."

Charlie concentrated on gluing, not sure what to say. Then, "Why did he have a teapot?"

"He didn't, silly. It's my teapot. Arthur bought it for me with his first week's wages for making cheese at the farm. Only fifteen he was and us on a day trip to Southport. He was sweet on me even then, you see. Nineteen twenty-five. Seems like yesterday. Seven pence, that's what it cost."

Charlie gasped, "But it's nearly a hundred years ago."

Mrs Tyrer folded her arms and lifted her chin,

"Why so it is. So now you're wondering how old I am, I suppose."

Charlie didn't say anything.

"I was born in nineteen-ten, so work it out for yourself."

"Ninety," said Charlie quickly. "Wow!" He'd never known anyone that old.

"I'm glad they still teach you arithmetic," said Mrs Tyrer, "and don't rely on those new-fangled thingummybobs."

"Calculators? We use those too."

"Didn't have those in my day – nor televisions or these recorder things."

"You had radios though."

20

"Some did, some didn't. My old ma never had a stove."

"So how did she cook?"

"Over the fire – and in the oven alongside the fire. Ever had toast from a toasting fork, Charlie, spread with home-churned butter?"

"No."

"Don't know what you've missed."

Charlie held the last piece in place and took a deep breath. He wanted to ask Mrs Tyrer about the girl in the picture, about the war. Instead, he said. "Who made the mouse?"

"I have no idea," said Mrs Tyrer. "It must have been in the teapot. I found it on the floor when I was sweeping up."

"I like it."

She looked at him thoughtfully and made a little grunting sound, as if she had made up her mind about something.

"You can have it if you like," she said. "Arthur must have found it and put it there. Never threw anything away if he thought it might come in useful."

"Are you sure? I do like it, although it's a funny looking thing." Charlie put it in his pocket. "It can be my lucky mouse," he said, laughing.

"Good idea," said Mrs Tyrer. "He probably found it on his way home from work. He worked at the shoe factory, you see, after the war. Always finding things was Arthur. Always looking, that was his trouble. Found a ten-shilling note once, and a sovereign years ago when he was just a lad. What a find that was."

"There," said Charlie, standing the teapot on the other side of the table to look at it. "It's not very good, is it? You can see all the joins."

"It's a bit like me," said Mrs Tyrer, laughing again. "It'll do. You've made a good job of it Charlie Pringle. Now I suppose you want paying."

Charlie shook his head.

She frowned and looked sideways at him. "Isn't that why you came, to earn a bit of pocket money? There's nothing wrong with that."

"Yes, but I haven't done anything yet – except break Arthur's teapot. Anyway, you have paid me. You gave me the mouse."

And this time they both laughed.

"Would you like a cup of tea? I haven't any pop or such."

"Yes please," said Charlie, "and I'll make it. I'm a dab hand at making tea."

"Shall I pay you for that then?"

"No," said Charlie.

"This is for free – on one condition."

Mrs Tyrer pretended to be shocked.

"You're old enough to help me with my homework. We're doing some history stuff and I need someone to interview about the war. I don't know anyone else who's old enough. Is tomorrow OK? I'll bring some paper and a pencil."

"I should think I'm nearly old enough to help Noah with his homework," said Mrs Tyrer, "but I shall have to put my thinking cap on."

Later, at home.

"Mum, who was General Eisenhower?"

"An American president, but I'm not sure when. Ask your dad. History wasn't my thing."

"During the war, I think," said his dad. "No, that was Roosevelt. Before my time, Son. Look in an encyclopaedia. That's why we bought them. We hoped you'd be cleverer than us."

"Is it homework?" asked his mum.

"Sort of. Mrs Tyrer said something about General Eisenhower and a bumblebee. I'm going to ask her tomorrow, but I thought I'd find out who he was first. How do you spell his name?"

"E. I. S. E. N. H. O. W. E. R."

Charlie soon found it in his encyclopaedia.

Dwight David Eisenhower, US General and 34th president. Supreme Commander for the 1944 cross-channel invasion of the continental mainland.

"Wow!" said Charlie. "Sounds like he was pretty important. Wouldn't it be great if Mrs Tyrer had a good story about him?" Charlie felt excited. He imagined it was the way explorers felt – or people like David Attenborough when they found something new, something that no one else had seen.

Most Saturday afternoons, Stephen Cropper came round and they went to the park to kick a ball around. Usually, it was all Charlie could think about but he had really enjoyed the history lessons this week and he was itching to find out more, especially as he now knew someone who had been a grown-up in the war.

His mum thought he was ill or had eaten something strange. Homework was never top of Charlie's list.

"Aren't you going out to play then?" she asked.

"Maybe."

"You ought to get some fresh air and exercise. It's not good to be stuck in here all day."

"You coming to the park?"

"Later, when I've done this ironing. I'll bring Mary-Lou down for a walk."

"Googoo!"

"And Googoo of course."

They heard a voice down below shouting up, "You coming, Charlie?" It was Stephen Cropper. When Charlie looked out, he saw Stephen and two other boys, Wesley and Tim, kicking a ball up against Mrs Tyrer's wall. It was what they always did. Charlie raced down the stairs just in time to hear the ball smash against the window. He saw the curtain move and thought about Mrs Tyrer.

One of the other boys snatched up the ball and ran. It was all part of the game to them. Charlie ran after them. What else could he do? He hoped she hadn't seen him. He wanted to say something, to tell them about Mrs Tyrer and how old she was and that she'd been alive in the war and that she knew a famous general – and that she'd be worried about the window breaking. But he didn't.

Instead, he followed them to the park.

****

It was always fun, kicking the ball about, practising sharp moves and trying to smash it past Stephen and into the net. Charlie might not have been very tall but he was quick and could change direction like a bird or a mouse. When they'd had enough and were all out of puff, they sat on the swings and talked about the best footballers – and what they were having for Christmas and what they were going to be when they grew up.

Stephen Cropper said he was going to be a businessman like his dad, but he was going to make even more money than his dad and have a bigger car. The other two, Wesley and Tim, both wanted to be footballers and live in mansions like David Beckham.

Charlie said he wasn't sure yet. He wanted to climb Everest – and invent something, or discover something or go exploring in the rainforests.

"You're nuts," said Stephen. "There's spiders and snakes and stuff there. And who's going to pay you to do that?"

Charlie didn't know, but Wesley said people like that were on the telly, and they got paid lots of money.

"Perhaps I'll be an archaeologist," said Charlie.

"What's that?" said Tim.

"History and bones and stuff," said Wesley.

"Yuck!" said Tim, pretending to be sick.

"Or maybe a writer," said Charlie.

"Any of you done that homework yet?" asked Stephen. "About the war an' stuff."

"Nah!" said Tim. "Gavin says how I should make a story up. He said I should go to the library and find a book about the war. If I had a computer, I could look for something on the Internet."

Gavin was Tim's big brother. He'd been suspended from school for smoking and selling cigarettes to the little kids.

"You can't do that," said Charlie. "That's not proper history."

"Who cares?" said Tim.

Stephen was grinning. He thought it was a brilliant idea, though he didn't actually say so. "You'd soon get found out," he said, "because everyone can do the same thing."

"My gran's big sister worked in a factory making bombs," said Wesley. "She told my gran they were always scared in case the Germans dropped a bomb on the factory. They had to use all the railings from parks and things because they needed more bombs all the time and they hadn't got enough iron."

"So what are you doing, Charlie Farlie?" asked Stephen.

Charlie glared at him.

"Well, my granddad was a hero," said Stephen.

"He was in the RAF – and we've got photographs of him and his plane."

The others looked at him doubtfully.

"It's true," said Stephen. "He got shot down – and he was in the Battle of Britain."

"Is he dead, then?" asked Tim.

"Don't be a prat," said Wesley.

"He might be. Did he use a parachute?" asked Tim.

"He must've done, mustn't he?" said Stephen.

"My great-granddad was at Dunkirk," said Wesley. "He was rescued by a fishing boat and was in hospital for ages. He couldn't fight any more after that."

"My granddad never stopped until the end of the war," said Stephen. "He got a medal, too. He got lots of medals. My story's going to be brilliant. I bet I'm the only one in the class with a real hero in the family – and I've got a bit of shrapnel they took out of his leg. Everyone says I look like my granddad."

Tim and Wesley shrugged. They jumped off the swings and ambled away, dribbling the ball between them. Stephen was looking very pleased with himself.

"So what are you going to do, Charlie? You still haven't said."

"That's because I don't know, not properly."

Then Charlie spotted his mum and Mary-Lou coming into the park. He waved and his mum waved back.

"Do you like having a sister?"

"It's OK."

"But she's still a baby. You can't have any fun with her. I'm glad I haven't got one. Do they like her better than you?"

"Don't be daft!"

"I bet she's got more toys."

"That's cos she's only little. People buy her stuff."

"I bet she'll have a bike when she gets older."

"I'm having a bike for Christmas – and a football – and maybe even a microscope."

Charlie knew immediately that he shouldn't have said that.

"What do you want a *microscope* for? We might be going skiing," said Stephen Cropper. "My mum doesn't like cooking Christmas dinner."

"I don't think I'd like to do that," said Charlie.

"You're only saying that because you can't."

"No, I'm not. Come on," said Charlie, "let's play some more. I'll be in goal. Hey, you two, come on. I'm in goal now."

****

On Sunday morning, Charlie knocked on Mrs Tyrer's door. He took two pencils and an exercise book with him so that he could be like a reporter, as long as she didn't talk too fast.

As usual, she peeped at him with the chain in place before she let him in. She seemed pleased to see him.

"Haven't you got any children?" he asked.

"Not a one," she replied.

"What about brothers and sisters?"

"All gone except me, and me the eldest."

Charlie was surprised at how cheerful she sounded. He didn't know that when you were ninety, it was wonderful if someone said they needed your help. She already had the kettle on and there was a plate of Jammie Dodgers on the table.

"So, Charlie Pringle, how can I help you with your homework?"

"I have to write a story," said Charlie, "about the war. Only it has to be true. It's supposed to be something your granddad did, but mine was too young and I haven't got any great-grandparents. Can I ask you a question?"

"Isn't that why you're here?"

He grinned.

"I tell you what," said Mrs Tyrer. "We'll make a cup of tea. Then I'll pretend to be a really interesting person and you can interview me like they do on the telly."

"OK."

So that's what they did.

"Right," said the old lady, a cup of tea on her lap. "Fire away. First question."

"The photograph in the china cabinet, the girl in the nurse's uniform with the soldiers. Is that you?"

"It is. I know, hard to believe. I can't believe it myself sometimes. She looks so young, so alive and beautiful. That was in Berlin, 1945."

"But that's in Germany, isn't it?"

"Yes, but the war had ended and the Allies were moving into Berlin to sort things out. I went in with lots of other nurses to look after the wounded. Americans, Germans, British. It didn't matter who they were. They were all just boys to us and we treated them all the same. I remember when some oranges came for the British boys. There were none for the German prisoners of war, of course, but our boys shared them with everyone." She smiled at the memory and sipped her tea. "I never smell an orange without thinking of them, how kind and brave they all were – and some of them so very young."

Charlie frowned. Oranges weren't very exciting. He was thinking of Stephen Cropper, bragging about his granddad's medals.

"What was the most exciting thing that happened?"

Mrs Tyrer thought for a moment. "Now that's a difficult question. Exciting for me at the time – or exciting for you now?"

"Both, I suppose," said Charlie.

"It was all exciting in a way," she said. "It was dangerous and scary and heart-breaking at times and you had to work very hard, but still, it was exciting. Because until the war came most young people had hardly been anywhere, not like young folks today with cars and money and trips abroad. The war gave them opportunities to see a bit more of the world and do things they had never dreamed of doing."

"But it was dangerous!"

"Of course it was, but it was still exciting, to begin with, anyway. And you knew that whatever happened you were doing your bit for your country and your boys. You just got on with it and did what you had to do. It was the mothers I always thought about, waiting at home for that terrible telegram to arrive."

"What's a telegram? Is it just like a letter?"

"It was a short message that was sent immediately from a contraption in one post office to another. Like on the telephone. Then the postman delivered it. I've got one here somewhere. My sister's husband, Stanley, died in a Japanese POW camp. They'd only been married four days when he went away, and she never saw him again."

"Was he killed?"

"No. He died of dysentery. That's a terrible illness people get when they live in dreadful conditions and don't have proper food."

Charlie thought for a moment.

"Did I tell you that as well as a story we need to take things in, things from the war, like?"

"No, you didn't. But I suppose you'd like the telegram – and maybe a photograph of Stanley's grave."

"Yes, please. I'd look after them."

"I'll have to find them first. I've got a carnation from the King."

"Is that a good story?"

"Yes, but it's not a war story. That was before the war."

"What about General Eisenhower?"

"That was right at the end of the war, Charlie Pringle." She sat sipping her tea and staring at something Charlie couldn't see.

30

"Are you OK?"

Mrs Tyrer nodded and smiled at something in the distance, something Charlie couldn't see. "I'll tell you about the King, shall I?" she said, and her face lit up. It was quite clear she was dying to. "I was at Sandringham, staying for the weekend."

"I've heard of Sandringham. What is it?"
"One of the royal houses."

Charlie frowned. What was Mrs Tyrer doing in the King's house? Was she making it all up, teasing him? Or was she a bit fuddled? Charlie's mum said his own grandma was a bit fuddled at times and she wasn't as old as Mrs Tyrer.

But Mrs Tyrer knew what he was thinking. Her eyes twinkled. "I was in service," she said, "working for Lord Trenchard, the Commissioner of Police. I helped his wife around the house and looked after the children. That's before I trained as a Red Cross nurse. King George the fifth had invited them to Sandringham with lots of other important people for the weekend. But there was a problem. You see, they didn't have pots of money like lots of the other guests. They couldn't afford a lady's maid and a chauffeur. So Lord Trenchard's sergeant was chauffeur for the weekend and yours truly was lady's maid."

Mrs Tyrer placed her cup and saucer on the table. Her hand shook and the cup rattled. Then she got up stiffly and went across to a chest of drawers. She tugged at one of the drawers but it didn't open so Charlie went to help her and together they almost pulled the drawer onto the floor. Inside there were towels and tea towels and snowy-white antimacassars and doilies, all neatly folded. She lifted some of them aside and pulled out a book that looked like an old diary. Back in her chair, she opened the diary and lifted out something wrapped in cellophane. She put it on the table and carried on with her story.

"When the weekend was over, Sergeant Bob and I took the car round to collect Lord and Lady Trenchard. That's when I saw the King."

"What was his name?" Charlie got mixed up with kings and queens. It seemed there had been so many of them.

"King George the fifth, the queen's grandfather. He was standing on the steps with his footman – and his footman was holding a big bunch of red carnations. As each lady took her leave of him, he presented her with a single carnation. What a lovely idea, don't you think? Such a kind man. Well of course, I was watching – probably staring with my mouth wide open. I mean it's not every day you get so close to the King. You'll never guess what happened next."

"He told you off for staring. Mum says it's rude to stare."

"He did not! Quite the opposite in fact. He knew that cats can look at kings and didn't mind at all. He looked straight at me and smiled. Then he spoke to his footman, and the footman came down the steps in his wonderful livery, bowed to me and presented me, Edith Hughes, with a beautiful red carnation. I felt like a real lady."

Charlie looked at the small, brown, cabbage-looking thing on the table.

"And you kept it," he said, "just like Arthur's teapot – to remind you."

Mrs Tyrer smiled. "A carnation from the King," she said.

"Doesn't look much like a flower now," said Charlie.

"No, it doesn't, does it?" said the old lady. "But the memory of it is as fresh as a daisy."

"It's a good story," said Charlie.

"But it's not really what you want, is it?"

Charlie shook his head. "I shall write it down anyway," he said, "so that I can remember it too."

Mrs Tyrer began to push herself up from her chair, quite forgetting the diary on her knee. It fell to the floor and Charlie jumped up to retrieve it for her, as he knew she couldn't bend down. On the floor was a photograph, fallen from the pages. It was of a man in uniform. *RAF*, Charlie thought. He couldn't help asking. "Is that Arthur?"

The man looked young and strong and handsome, a bit like one of those old film stars his grandma liked, Gary Grant, or something.

"No," said Mrs Tyrer. "That's not Arthur. That's Guy."

She held the photograph to her and sank back into her chair. The sparkle had quite gone out of her eyes.

"Shall I make another cup of tea?" offered Charlie. It was his mum's remedy for everything, and his grandma's. He didn't know what else to say.

"Yes," said Mrs Tyrer, "that would be nice."

When Charlie came back into the room she seemed to be asleep. For one horrible, terrifying moment, Charlie wondered ... but then her hand moved – and he breathed again. She lifted the photograph and touched it to her face. Then she smiled and opened her eyes. Charlie saw tears glistening in the creases of her crumpled cheeks.

He put her cup and saucer on the table.

"Sorry, Charlie Pringle," she said. "Just a bit tired. Haven't talked so much in ages. I'll be right as rain tomorrow, you see."

"Are you sure?"

"Of course I'm sure. Not ready to turn my toes up yet, not till I've told you about the General – and Princess Mary and the Canadian who ate all the cakes. I hardly got any sleep last night thinking about them all."

"Wow! It sounds like 'Alice in Wonderland'," said Charlie.

"I felt like Alice in Wonderland sometimes," said Mrs Tyrer.

"Bye then," said Charlie.

"Can I come tomorrow, after school?"

"Four-thirty," said Mrs Tyrer. "I'll put the kettle on."

****

In school the next day, Mrs Taylor asked everyone how they were getting on with their research. She made them feel like real reporters, hunting for good stories to make the headlines. In fact, she said they would make them into a newspaper and choose the very best for the front page. So they wanted a good headline, something to catch everyone's attention.

"HERO NOSEDIVES INTO THE CHANNEL AND SURVIVES," wrote Stephen Cropper on the blackboard when Mrs Taylor wasn't looking. And when Stephen wasn't looking, Tim put the word DRUNK in front of hero.

"Very funny!" said Mrs Taylor, reappearing from the cupboard and picking up the board duster. "What about you, Charlie? What have you found out?"

Before Charlie could answer, Stephen Cropper piped up with, "None of his family was in the war, Miss. They're dead boring. He hasn't got any stories, but I've got a brilliant one."

"Good. Have you written it in your homework book?"

"Not yet, Miss."

"Well, when you have, you can read it to us." She glanced at Charlie to see if he had anything to say. But Charlie wasn't saying anything yet. He wasn't sure whether he'd have a war story or not.

"What about interesting objects? Has anyone found anything?"

"I've got two ration books," said Melanie Thomas, proudly.

"And I've got a bit of German aeroplane," said Michael Morris. "My Granddad found it in a field and my dad said he'd bring it in."

"S'probably just a bit of old tractor or something," said Stephen.

"Wonderful," said Mrs Taylor, ignoring him.

"Anything else?"

"I've got a cigarette case with a bullet mark on it," said Millie Spencer.

"Goodness!" said Mrs Taylor. "I bet that could tell a good story. It might have saved someone's life."

Millie smiled. Her Granddad had found it with a metal detector. It had a German name on it – and what looked like a bullet mark. Perhaps she could make up a story and no one would notice the German name. "Yes, Miss," she said. "It's my granddad's."

"My great-granddad's got five medals, Mrs Taylor," said Peter Baxter. "He was in the Engineers."

"My granddad's got six medals," said Stephen, not to be outdone by anyone, especially not wimpy Peter Baxter, "and one of them's a really good one."

"Is it a Victoria Cross?" asked Mrs Taylor.

"Probably," said Stephen, frowning. He'd heard of a Victoria Cross but he didn't know what it was exactly.

"Now that *would* be something special," said Mrs Taylor. "And it's given me an idea for another job for you. See what you can find out about medals and why they were given, especially the Victoria Cross. Then, when we've seen some, we can put our heads together and design our own medal for all the people whose stories we are going to write down."

Stephen grinned smugly at everyone. He'd got a brilliant idea and he was determined that his story was going to be the best.

As long as Charlie could remember, Stephen Cropper had come first in everything. He was good at football, the star of the team, though his dad rarely came to watch him, and Charlie's dad always came to the matches. Stephen could draw – and work sums out quickly in his head. He could write good stories too when he bothered to try – and he could even sing, though he was embarrassed about it. Charlie often wondered why they were friends – they lived in different parts of town – but he guessed it was because Stephen was so clever and Charlie desperately wanted to be. It was as if there were stars twinkling all around Stephen and Charlie was trying to touch them, hoping some of their sparkle would stick to him. He had always been used to Stephen beating him at everything. Mum and Dad said it didn't matter as long as you did your best, but sometimes it did matter, like now. Charlie didn't know what was different this time.

He just knew that it was. He knew that Mrs Tyrer, old Mrs Tyrer, living on her own, was every bit as good and brave and interesting as Stephen Cropper's granddad who had flown a fighter plane. And he wanted to tell everyone about it.

So, at four-thirty on the dot, he was knocking at her door again. She never opened it straight away, but always checked before she took off the chain.

"Can't be too careful these days," she told him sadly, and he wondered about the days when she was a girl and no one bothered to lock the door.

The teapot was sitting on an iron trivet in the middle of the table and there were four custard creams arranged neatly on a flowered plate.

"Does your mum mind you coming here?"

"No, why should she?"

"Strange company for a young man like you. Wouldn't you rather be playing football?" She looked at him sharply, her eyes twinkling.

"I do play football, but not in the dark. I'm not allowed anyway."

"So what's it to be today? Eisenhower, Belsen, Princess Mary, Dunkirk – or the spy on the train?"

Her old eyes blinked at him and Charlie remembered the face of the young pretty girl she had once been. It was the first time he had really understood that inside an old person, there must still be a young one. Charlie decided he didn't want to grow old.

"General Eisenhower, please," he said. "I've been finding out about him."

"He was a real sweetie. I bet your books didn't tell you that."

"No. They don't put things like that in history books and encyclopaedias."

"I was in Berlin with the Red Cross. We had followed the soldiers through Belgium and into Germany at the end of the war and General Eisenhower had come across to visit the American troops. He knew all about the good work being done by the Red Cross and he wanted to invite two Red Cross nurses to lunch."

"And one of them was you?"

"Yes, wasn't I lucky? I always tried to look smart, you see. Even though washing clothes was difficult – there was never enough soap or hot water – I always had a sparkling white uniform. It was important to me, and everyone said my smile was as bright as my uniform. So I suppose that's why I was chosen. Appearance isn't everything, Charlie Pringle, but it's what other people see first, and it tells them something about you, how much you care and how hard you work."

Mrs Tyrer took a deep breath and a sip of tea before she began again.

"We wore white gloves, too – and capes. I can't remember if it was Dolly Hesketh or May Phillips, who came with me. Anyway, we were walking under some trees, feeling very nervous. General Eisenhower was sitting at a table on the lawn with lots of other people around. He was going to make a speech about the Red Cross and the debt owed to them, but just as we got near a huge bumblebee landed on the back of my neck. I swiped at it – and it stuck to my glove.

When I shook it, the glove and the bumblebee flew through the air and landed on a plate of sandwiches smack in front of the General. I was horrified. There I was trying to look cool and efficient as always and only managed to make a fool of myself again."

"What happened next?"

"They laughed. Everyone did. They fell about. Someone nearly choked, so Dolly and I, (yes, I remember, it was Dolly), had to do some first aid. The General forgot all about his speech – and when we saw what a sweetie he was, we weren't nervous any more. It really broke the ice and we had a lovely lunch."

"Clever bumblebee," said Charlie.

"Yes, wasn't he?"

"What did you talk about?"

"This and that, I suppose. The end of the war, going home. What we would do afterwards."

"What *did* you do afterwards?"

"I went to Scotland to say goodbye to someone, someone I had met before the war."

"The man in the photograph?"

She smiled wistfully and nodded.

"How did you know that?"

Charlie shrugged. "But you didn't marry him?"

"No, I didn't marry him."

"Who was Princess Mary?"

"The King's sister."

"Did you have lunch with her too?"

"No, but I took tea with her one afternoon in the grounds of Windsor Castle."

"Is that when someone ate all the cakes?"

"No. That was another day. This time I went with five other nurses to have tea with Princess Mary and we were all very polite. We had cucumber sandwiches and sponge cake and scones – and we were on our very best behaviour, I can tell you. No, the greedy gannet who ate all the cakes was a Canadian. They were a dreadful unruly lot, no manners at all. That was after Dunkirk. We took all the head and spinal injuries at St Hugh's. He must have been very hungry, don't you think? We'd taken him to a little teashop in Oxford. It was part of our duty, you see, wheeling them around to keep up their spirits. We were only supposed to have one cake each. Things like that were rationed because of the sugar and butter shortages."

"But he ate six?"

"Every time we turned our heads another one disappeared."

"Perhaps he hadn't had any cakes since before the war."

"That's no excuse for bad manners."

"They must have been very good cakes."

Mrs Tyrer smiled.

"We had a little girl to tea once," said Charlie. "She was mum's friend's little girl. When nobody was looking she ate a whole bowl of tomatoes, but she was only little. Mum didn't mind. We all laughed."

Mrs Tyrer smiled at both their memories.

"That was the day I met the gardener. I mean, the day I was at Windsor Castle. Do you know, I had forgotten all about that. You're a tonic, you are, Charlie Pringle. I haven't had so much fun in years."

"What gardener?"

"The King's gardener. He told me a lovely story. Do you want to hear it?"

Charlie nodded. What else could he do? And Mrs Tyrer smiled.

"Apparently, King George the fifth had been given a beautiful shrub by someone in another country. I can't remember who. At least, it would be beautiful when it flowered. Every year, his gardener tended it and prayed it would flower in the King's lifetime. But it never did. Then, when the old King died and Edward became king, it produced a single bloom. The gardener was delighted, but sorry that his King had not lived to see it. The new king, on seeing the bloom, immediately cut it off to give to his lady friend, without a thought for the gardener who had tended it with such loving care. The next year, it bloomed again and now his brother, King George the sixth, was on the throne. He knew how the gardener had cherished the shrub and said that the blooms were far more beautiful in the garden than they could ever be in a vase. 'So you see,' the old man told me, 'we got the right man for king'."

"What happened to the other king?"

"He abdicated, gave up the throne of England so that he could marry the woman he loved."

"Oh. Love. Soppy stuff."

Mrs Tyrer smiled. "Next question," she said.

"What was the other one you said yesterday?"

"I don't remember. I've slept since then. You'll have to remind me."

"It began with a B. Bell something. I've forgotten its name. It was a Concentration Camp, wasn't it?"

"Belsen. Do you know what Belsen was, then?"

"Mrs Taylor told us a little bit. Did you go there?"

"Yes, I did ... but I don't think you want to hear about that, not yet. When you're older maybe."

"Was it very terrible?"

But Mrs Tyrer looked tired and sad. Then she stared again, at something far away, something half a century away.

"Two miles," she whispered. "Can you believe it? Two miles away and you could smell it."

"What?" asked Charlie. "What could you smell?"

"Death, Charlie Pringle, you could smell death, the most terrible smell on earth."

****

"So how was General Eisenhower?" asked Charlie's mum later.

Charlie grinned. "He was a sweetie. That's what she said. It was a good story but not a proper war story. I've still got to find one of those."

That evening, it seemed the moon was beckoning to him, shining directly through his bedroom window. Charlie knelt on his chair. The moon-ship must have changed course since the other night and there was no longer a silken-sailed barge sliding down the canal. But the dark moon shadows were still lingering around the bushes on the towpath – and in the factory yard – and there was that shadow again, drifting towards the gate – only this time it seemed bigger.

43

Then the window misted up with his close breathing and when Charlie cleared it with his sleeve, the shadow had gone from the yard. But there was another movement, outside the gate this time. Just for a second, Charlie saw it, and it looked for all the world like a boy pulling a cart.

                    ****

The next day, after school, Charlie called at a flower shop called 'Buds 'n Blooms'. He waited until Stephen had gone. He didn't want the others making fun of him. He'd asked his mum for some pocket money in advance and promised to help with the washing up. But the flowers were so expensive. He asked the lady for something that smelled really nice and she sold him a tiny bunch of freesias. They didn't look much but they did smell nice and she said they would last a long time.

As he was coming out of the shop, Stephen and his mum went past in the car. They had to slow down for some traffic lights and Stephen wound down the window and shouted, "Hiya, Charlie. What yer doing?"

Charlie thrust the flowers behind his back and waved with his other hand. Then he turned and walked in the opposite direction until the lights had changed. After tea, he ran downstairs to Number Two.

"I've brought you some flowers, Mrs Tyrer. They smell really nice. I can't stay tonight because we've got to go to my nana's, but I'll see you tomorrow, if that's OK."

"Can't you come in just for a moment?"

Charlie hesitated. His mum had said five minutes and no more.

"Just for a minute then."

On the table in the living room were shoeboxes full of old photographs. Some were stacked in small heaps. It looked like she'd been sorting through them. Charlie's eyes moved over the table and came to rest on a row of medals in small open boxes.

Mrs Tyrer took the flowers from him and sniffed them. "Freesias," she said. "My favourites. Now how did you know that, Charlie Pringle? It's a long time since anyone brought me flowers."

"Shall I put them in water for you?"

"They won't harm for a moment. I'll see to them when you've gone." She'd seen him looking at the medals. "You can pick them up," she said. "They won't break. One of them's made of bronze. It's a bit special is that one."

"Is it – a Victoria Cross?"

Mrs Tyrer nodded. "Clever boy."

"Is it Arthur's?"

She shook her head.

"The man in the photograph? What was his name?"

"Guy. The man in the photograph is Guy."

Charlie picked up the cross. 'For Valour,' it said on the front and it was attached to a dark red ribbon.

Then a knock came at the door and Charlie's mum shouted him.

"Oh dear," said Mrs Tyrer. "I hope you won't get into trouble. Will I see you tomorrow?"

"Yes – no. Oh shoot! We're going Christmas shopping. I'll see you Thursday, if that's OK."

45

"Yes," she said, "Thursday's fine. It'll give me time to find the letter, the official report."

"What do you mean, Mrs Tyrer?"

"Guy and the Victoria Cross," she said, "and the other things you were wanting, the telegram and the photo. I'll have such a time looking for them."

She nodded and smiled as he made his way out. "Thank you for the flowers, Charlie Pringle." And then she kissed him. Charlie fled. He thought he would probably rather be thumped than kissed. Still, you had to make sacrifices for your friends sometimes, and Mrs Tyrer smelled of lavender, which was quite nice in a weird, old-fashioned sort of way.

Just as she was closing the door on him, Charlie stopped and turned around. "Mrs Tyrer," he said, quietly, in case anyone else was around, "Do you believe in ghosts?"

The old lady smiled and lifted her shoulders.

"Why do you ask?"

"Have you ever *seen* a ghost?"

"Perhaps. Have you?"

There was a strange look on Mrs Tyrer's face as if she knew something he didn't. As Charlie turned to go she whispered conspiratorially, "You mean the boy in the yard. I did wonder how long it would be before you saw him too, you living at Number Twenty-Six ..."

"You've seen him too?"

"Charlie! Do hurry or we'll miss the bus."

Charlie was burning to ask her more but there was no time.

"You have seen him, haven't you? Wow! Got to go, sorry. See you Thursday."

In school the next day, after maths, Stephen Cropper was the first to read out his story.

He stood up grandly and began, "My grandfather, Flight-Lieutenant Samuel Cropper was on patrol over Southampton in a Hurricane ... That's an aeroplane," explained Stephen, "not a storm ... He decided to chase a Junkers ..."

"What's that?"

"A German plane, you moron, the best bomber they had.

"...when suddenly, this Messerschmitt comes from nowhere and is right on his tail. Before he could dodge it, the Messerschmitt had fired four cannons into his plane ... One hit him in the eye, another smashed into the front of the plane, another hit a petrol tank and set the plane on fire and the last one hit him in the foot so there was blood everywhere and the plane was melting.

"His hands were burnt and all the controls were melting like candles but he still kept the plane up though he was in agony, and he kept firing and firing at the German plane. He didn't stop until he shot it down and it crashed into the English Channel. Then he tried to get out of his burning plane but his seat belt got stuck and he had to pull it and he was nearly unconscious so he was doing it all wrong.

Then he managed to do it just in time, before the plane exploded.

"He dived head first and did lots of somersaults through the air. He almost tied himself in knots. Then he got straightened out and floated down.

But then another Messerschmitt came so he just sort of flopped and pretended to be dead so they wouldn't shoot at him ... and he landed in a field with eighty bits of metal in him."

" ... And that was just the first time he got shot down. Once, he ended up in the English Channel and was floating about for two days before a fishing boat found him. But he kept on flying until the end of the war, and the Germans never managed to kill him. He's got six medals. But we don't know where they are."

"What a wonderful story," said Mrs Taylor and Stephen's face lit up. "Your granddad must have had nine lives." She was really pleased with him, and the children in class were on the edges of their seats as he told of his granddad's exploits.

"What an excellent start," said the teacher. "We have a brilliant journalist in our midst. I hope Stephen has inspired the rest of you to produce interesting stories. Now, anything else to report before I tell you about life in the countryside for our little evacuees – or 'vackies', as they were called? Has anyone found a Victoria Cross yet?"

"I'm sure my granddad must have got one," said Stephen, still glowing. "But no one knows where it is. We'll have to look for it."

Charlie looked around, hoping that someone else had a hero in the family. But no one did, at least, not yet. Then Charlie's hand shot up of its own accord, before his brain had time to rethink and object. He wouldn't let Stephen Cropper do everything better than him. He just wouldn't.

Mrs Taylor smiled, "Yes, Charlie?"

"I know someone who's got one, Miss. I've seen it."

"Really? Are you sure? They are quite rare, you know. Only 1,354 have been awarded in a 150 years."

"There was one on the 'Antiques Roadshow'," said Tim. "They're worth a lot of money."

"That wasn't a Victoria Cross! It was something else!"

"You don't watch that!"

"Boring!"

"My mum does."

"So does mine. Then she goes looking in the attic in case there's something valuable hidden up there, like a painting or something."

"And all she finds is spiders."

"It's made out of bronze," said Charlie.

"And what do you know about that?" asked Mrs Taylor.

Charlie glanced around. No one else had done his homework. Not even Stephen Cropper. But Charlie had. As soon as they'd got back from Nana's last night, he'd looked in his encyclopaedia.

"Up until 1942," he said, "they were made from the bronze that came from the captured Russian cannons."

"Cannon," said Mrs Taylor, "the plural of cannon is cannon. – And which war was that?"

"The Crimean War," said Charlie, "in 1850 something. A hundred and fifty years ago when we were fighting against Russia."

"Well done, Charlie. So, are you going to tell us who was awarded this wonderful medal?"

"I'm not sure yet," said Charlie.

"You don't know anyone!" shouted Stephen.

"I do," said Charlie. "There's this old lady I know. She's a friend – and it must be one of her relatives, because she's got lots of medals – and lots of stories. She was a nurse and she went to Berlin and Belsen and she met General Eisenhower and the King and the Princess. She's just an ordinary person but she's done lots of exciting things."

"I'd like to meet her," said Mrs Taylor.

"Does she live close to you?"

Charlie nodded. "At number two." But he was already wishing he hadn't said so much. He didn't want everyone else to know Mrs Tyrer. He just wanted to keep her stories for himself, for the moment, anyway.

"Do you think she might come in to see us?"

"I don't know. She doesn't go out much. Someone does her shopping for her. She's very old."

"OK. Well, you get your stories written down, and then we'll see. Perhaps we can write a letter to her and ask her politely. Now, let's get on."

 ****

"I saw you with those soppy flowers," said Stephen later. "And guess what. We came past your place this morning, and I looked for you, and what did I see, flowers – in the old biddy's window, that naggy old bat who always bangs at us when we play football. So that's where you've been going. Doesn't look much like a hero to me. What could she do in the war? Is that the best you can find, Charlie Farlie? I bet you made it all up anyway."

"That's cheating, that is," said Tim, pulling a face. "Not proper history. Old ladies don't get given medals anyway."

"You don't know anything," said Charlie angrily.

"And she wasn't old in the war, was she, you prat? Anyway it's not her medal. It's someone else's, someone who's dead."

"They're just jealous," said Wesley. "Take no notice, Charlie. Stephen's in a bad mood 'cos his mum and dad are making him go to his grandma's for Christmas."

"He said they were going skiing."

"*They are* – but *he's* not. My mum said."

            ****

After tea, Charlie and his mum and dad and Mary-Lou caught the bus into the town centre. While his mum and dad were looking at toys for Mary-Lou, Charlie crept away to look at the mountain bikes. He knew which one he wanted. It was black and silver and had Magura brakes. He kept an eye on his mum and dad so they wouldn't see him looking. He knew they would buy him a bike if they could and take him somewhere out in the countryside so he could ride some trails and have fun off-road like he'd seen them doing on the telly. "One day," he said to himself, "one day."

He'd decided to buy a Christmas present for Mrs Tyrer. She had no one to buy her presents. But what could you buy for such an old lady? Chocolate biscuits, more flowers – or something scented to put in the bath? He would have to think about it.

When the pushchair was hung with bags, dad took them all for a milkshake to pass time until the next bus. While they sat waiting, some boys went past, kicking a can. They weren't supposed to do that in the precinct. There was usually a policeman about. But Charlie knew what would happen if a policeman came into sight. The boys would leave the can and run off in different directions. It was easy for kids to dodge through the crowds and not so easy for a grown-up. They almost never got caught.

"Isn't that Tim's brother?" said Charlie's mum. Charlie nodded.

"They shouldn't be doing that," said his dad. "It's dangerous for little kids and old people."

Then Gavin Smedley spotted Charlie. Charlie didn't like him. He wasn't like Tim. Tim was a bit dim, but he was harmless enough. Gavin grinned. It wasn't a friendly grin, but more of a 'see what I'm doing' sort of grin – an 'I don't give a toss' sort of grin and a 'see who's out with his mummy and daddy' sort of grin. But when he looked at Charlie, he took his eye off what he was doing for a moment and crashed into an elderly lady, knocking her against a shop window.

Charlie's dad rushed to help her, but Gavin had fled. She was OK, she said, just winded and a little shaky. Boys will be boys. She'd be all right after a drink and a sit down.

"I'll report the little hooligan," said Charlie's dad, angrily.

Then a policeman appeared from somewhere and Charlie's dad was telling him what had happened. "Not safe for decent folk," he said, "especially old ones. They'll be afraid of coming out through the door if we don't do something."

Charlie's dad hadn't seen Gavin watching them, but Charlie had. There was a bookstand outside a shop and Gavin was behind it, waiting to see if they had reported him. Convinced that they had, he lifted his hand and pointed a finger meaningfully at Charlie. Then he coolly stuffed a book inside his anorak and walked away.

Charlie's dad hadn't admitted to knowing Gavin. He wouldn't want his son to be visited by a policeman, not if there was another more private way of dealing with it. Gavin hadn't exactly committed a crime, but the boy needed speaking to. He would go around there and have a word with his parents.

"Did you tell him, Dad? Did you give him Gavin's name?"

"No, Son, I didn't."

"He thinks you did. I saw him. I could tell by the look on his face."

"Well, I didn't, and that's all that matters. I'll go round and have a word with him. I know his dad. Then that'll be an end to it. The boy just wants educating."

But Charlie knew different. Gavin Smedley was not someone you messed with. He acted like he was sixteen.

****

"I missed you," said Mrs Tyrer on Thursday.

This time, Charlie noticed, she took the chain off and opened the door straightaway, without checking that it was Charlie.

The biscuits and tea were on the table. But the medals were nowhere to be seen, and the photograph and diary had been put away.

"So what is it to be today?" she asked. "Shall we have something jolly to cheer us up? It's lovely to chat."

She must have forgotten what she'd said about the Victoria Cross. Perhaps thinking about it had made her too sad. Charlie wasn't in need of cheering up – he needed a good story – but perhaps she was.

So, though he was dying to hear about a real hero, he said he really didn't mind. He liked all her stories and it didn't matter if they were about the war or not.

"Anything," he said, "whatever you want to tell me, and I shall write it down and put all your stories in a book and keep them."

"Well I never, Charlie Pringle. You're a treat, and no mistaking. So Edith Tyrer won't be quite forgotten when she goes?"

"Never," said Charlie, for he felt as though he had known her for ages. "Do you have any stories about Christmas?"

"What a good idea," she said. "There's Auntie Jinnie's box – or the Noah's Ark story. But that was after Christmas when the floods were up."

"Can we have both?" said Charlie.

"Pour the tea, then, there's a good boy."

Charlie was just passing a cup and saucer to Mrs Tyrer when something hit the window with a thud. They both jumped and the cup tipped over in the saucer. Charlie rushed into the kitchen for a cloth to clean up the spill before dashing to the window.

Gavin Smedley was standing outside on the square of grass. He was holding a ball under his arm. His other hand was holding tightly on to Tim's collar. Gavin grinned horribly when he saw Charlie pulling the curtain aside to look. Then he shook his head, turned and marched Tim away.

"Do you want me to go?" Charlie asked when the mess was cleared up and he'd made another cup of tea. He thought Mrs Tyrer must hate all boys.

"No need," said Mrs Tyrer. "I should be used to it by now. Heaven knows I've lived here long enough.

And they don't mean any real harm. They just don't understand how frightening life can become when you get old."

She sipped her tea for a few moments and Charlie nibbled on a biscuit, though it felt like sawdust.

"We'll not be put off," she said. "Chins up and thumbs up and fight back. That's what they said in the Blitz, and that's why we didn't let Hitler beat us. Now, back to Christmas." She wriggled comfortably into her chair and smoothed down her skirt. "There were four of us," she began, "children, that is. Two boys and two girls. I was the oldest. Then there was Bobbie and Winifred and Tom. We used to call our dad Old Joe when he wasn't around, pretending we weren't scared of him, but we were. He was big and he liked his beer and smokes – and his garden. Used to spend hours leaning on the gate into the lane, chatting to all and sundry as they passed. Always seemed to be a robin around him. Used to take worms from his hand.

And there was one there when he died, perched on the old stone.

"Joe was a builder, so when the weather was bad, there was no work. That's when times were hard. But Mother was wonderful. Busy and quick as a little starling, she was. No matter how hard times were, she always managed to put a decent meal on the table and visitors were always welcome. Course, we were a lot luckier than some. We had a few chickens and four cows and a garden and an orchard with some apple trees and blackcurrant bushes. So there were always eggs and milk and jam."

"You didn't live in a town then?"

"Oh no. Bless you, I'm a country girl, born and bred. And Arthur was a country boy. Can't remember how we ended up here. Something to do with his job. I used to live at Number Twenty-Six, you know, till the stairs got too much."

"But that's where I live."

"I know."

Mrs Tyrer twisted in her chair and pointed at the china cabinet. "See that little pink jug. Mother used to fill it with whisky at Christmas and it was passed around the table so everyone could have a drop in their tea. A rare treat, that was. Still, though we had enough to eat, there was no money for things like toys and decorations and such, not like today."

"Did you have a Christmas tree?"

"In a fashion, though not like you do now. On Christmas Eve, when we children had disappeared up the wooden hills, Mother would go out with a lamp and cut a branch of holly. Then she would tie it to one of the ceiling beams and decorate it with paper stars and bits of silver paper collected from cigarette packets and such. When we got up, she would already be in the kitchen and a great pudding would be steaming outside in the copper. The fire would be roaring away and the silver paper balls would be sparkling."

She smiled at the memory.

"Did you have a stocking?"

"We did, Old Joe's thick knitted boot socks, but there wasn't a great deal in them. A few nuts perhaps, and an apple or an orange. Maybe a sugar mouse and a small toy, or an old one mended."

"Is that all?"

"It would have been, except for Auntie Jinnie. Have you heard of fairy godmothers, Charlie Pringle?"

"Yes, there's one in Cinderella. I saw the pantomime last Christmas."

"Well, Auntie Jinnie was our fairy godmother. She was a wonderful cook and worked in grand houses all over the country. At Christmas, she filled a big box with treats and surprises for us all. Cakes, sweets she'd made, sugar mice and peppermint bars, nuts and crystallised fruits – and toys, wonderful, magical toys."

"What kind of toys?"

"The kind you were almost afraid to touch because they were so beautiful. Clockwork merry-go-rounds and Chinese pagodas with tiny people that seemed to come alive in the candlelight. You can imagine how eagerly we awaited the arrival of Auntie Jinnie's box."

Suddenly, Charlie had an idea that made him tingle, something he could do for Mrs Tyrer for Christmas.

"Yes," he said, "I can imagine. But you didn't open it before Christmas, did you?"

"Oh no. That would have been a hanging offence – or a good beating at least. But we stood looking at it and touching it, trying to picture what was inside."

The old lady and the boy, with almost a century between them, smiled at each other and said nothing for a few minutes. Mrs Tyrer was remembering those Christmases long ago when the world was very different; Charlie was trying hard to imagine it.

Then, "What about Noah's Ark?"

"It's only a little story," she said, "but then it was only a little boat, overladen, just like the Ark. And that's what we called it afterwards. Our Bobbie painted the name on the side."

"Whose boat was it?"

"Old Joe's. We lived near the Dee and many a year it flooded. Sometimes the floods froze and then we had skating parties. Folks were known to skate all the way to Chester on the river."

"But rivers don't freeze, do they? Not in this country."

"They did then, sure as eggs is eggs. I've seen it with my own eyes. Everyone had skates, even the poorest folk. It was great sport. We had such fun, such marvellous fun, skating in the moonlight, just like you see on those old Christmas cards." Her eyes sparkled at the memory. "Ee, Charlie Pringle. You've brought it all back. I haven't thought about that in years. What wonderful times I've had and no mistake.

Now, where was I?"

"Noah's Ark."

"Yes, of course. Noah's Ark. Old Joe had no work, on account of the weather, so was helping out, rescuing folks who were trapped by the floods. He'd been downriver to rescue an old couple from a cottage, but they refused to leave without all their animals. We were waiting on the bank for him to come back, and when we saw the boat, we laughed and laughed.

If I remember right, our Winifred wet herself. She was such a giggler. The boat was loaded to the gunnels and so low in the water, we thought it was going to sink.

There was Old Joe, William and Aggie Crump, four sheep, twelve hens, six ducks, two cats, a cockerel and a basketful of eggs. And you'll never guess where the old cockerel was perched. On Joe's head. Good job he had a cap on. And he was crowing for all he was worth, just like a town crier. Everyone cheered, and someone took a photo. It was in the newspaper."

"That's a good story."

"Do you know? I do believe I've still got some old diaries of my Mother's. She was always cutting out bits from newspapers and keeping them. I wonder if it's worth looking. It'll give me something to do before you come again. Isn't this exciting?"

Charlie grinned. Her face looked different now, younger, somehow, the wrinkles smoothed away. He could almost see the young girl inside. He nodded. *Yes, it is exciting. But you might forget,* he thought, *like you forgot about the Victoria Cross.* He wanted to say something, desperately. But suddenly the old lady looked tired. She'd got that faraway look again as if she'd gone back to those old days of skating on the river and candlelit Christmases – and Charlie felt he couldn't ask her.

"I'm sorry, Charlie Pringle," she said suddenly, when she seemed to have forgotten he was there. "You want to hear about Guy, don't you? I've never told anyone; do you know that? Not one single person.

Not even Arthur."

"Was Guy a real hero then?"

"Oh, yes, my dear, a real hero. And Arthur didn't want to know about soldiers and airmen, because Arthur couldn't fight in the war, you see. He'd had rheumatic fever as a boy and the best he could do was work in a munitions factory."

"So what did Guy do?"

"He flew a Hurricane, that's what he did. He'd been a farmer before, but in the war he flew a Hurricane."

Just like Stephen Cropper's granddad. Charlie waited. Mrs Tyrer sighed.

"If you don't want to tell me, it's OK. Honest," said Charlie.

She smiled and placed her hand on her heart. "I've kept him safe in here, you see," she said, "for all these years – and poor Arthur knew that. Tomorrow, Charlie Pringle, I'll give you such a story." Charlie nodded.

"I'll have the kettle on."

"And I'll bring some of mum's scones. Bye, Mrs Tyrer. See you tomorrow."

Then he remembered and simply had to ask. "What about the boy, Mrs Tyrer, the boy in the factory yard. Do you think he is a ghost?"

"I reckon he must be. Caught him looking up at the window many a time, but I don't think it was me he was looking for. Perhaps he's been looking for you, Charlie Pringle, all this time."

It was an alarming thought. "What for?" Charlie wasn't sure he liked that idea. "He doesn't look up at me. He doesn't even know I'm there. He just pulls a cart or something."

"An errand boy, I should think, doing odd jobs at the factory. Don't you fret about it now. I'm sure he means no harm. He's caught up in a sort of wrinkle, you know, a wrinkle in time, and he's waiting for someone to iron it out. A bit like you and me really. We're from quite different times aren't we? Think of it like this, Charlie Pringle. You are in one pool and I am in another. Our lives send out ripples, sometimes little ones and sometimes big ones – and sometimes those ripples reach out and touch each other and we get a glimpse of someone else's life and world and we are richer because of it."

"But you're real."

"So is he – just further away, I think."

"Can I talk to him then, like I talk to you?"

"Why not? He might have a story to tell you."

****

Charlie stayed up late that night, writing down Mrs Tyrer's stories properly before he forgot them. He even wrote down what she had said about the boy. Every now and again, he would get up and peer through the window. It was a cloudy night and the moon had all but disappeared. Occasionally, he would catch a glimpse of it where the cloud was thinner. Then it would vanish again.

The canal was in darkness till it caught a silver smudge of moonlight and glimmered briefly like a candle before a draught blew it out. He was glad he'd asked Mrs Tyrer about the ghost, if it was a ghost. He wasn't sure.

But then it must be, or else how would she have known what he had seen. She must have seen it when she lived at Number Twenty-Six. Perhaps she'd had a chair by the window like Charlie.

It had gone nine-thirty and Charlie had just put away his book. When he switched off the light and peeped through the curtain, the moon had moved on and was looking back at him through a hole in the cloud. It was the only light he could see. For although the factory was always in darkness, the yellow light from the town filtered through the air and up into the sky and nowhere was ever completely dark. Never, that is, until tonight.

Charlie wished he could open his window and look out, for everywhere seemed to be in utter darkness. Even the flats had no lights on. There were no pale glows from windows, no sounds of TVs – and no traffic. He looked at his clock. Nine-thirty-five. It wasn't that late, and there was always some traffic, even through the night. Then, as his eyes grew more accustomed to the dark, he saw a shadow, darker than the air, moving towards the factory gate, just like before. Only this time, it stopped and he could see that it was a boy. Even in the darkness, he could see him clearly. For a single sharp moment, the moon lit on his pale face and he was looking up, straight at Charlie. Mrs Tyrer had been right.

He couldn't wait to see her tomorrow, to find out what else she knew.

But when Charlie came home next day, Mary-Lou was sick. She had a temperature and a rash and Charlie's mum was out of her mind with worry.

As soon as Charlie got home, they got ready to dash half a mile to the surgery although the lady on the phone said not to worry, there was a bug going around.

"How can she tell us not to worry when we don't know what's wrong? It could be meningitis or something."

"I thought she'd had a jab for that."

"Yes, she has, but there are different kinds aren't there? Oh, I don't know, Charlie love. Where are my shoes? I can't find my shoes. Do you think we ought to get a taxi or just go?"

"Here they are," said Charlie. "I'll come with you, Mum. We can walk. It's only ten minutes."

"What about your dad? He won't be home for another hour, will he? It's Friday and he'll want his tea."

"We can leave him a note. He can come down after us if we're still not back."

"Of course we can. You do that, Charlie, love. Stick it on the breadboard. It's the first place he'll look when he comes in. Always goes to put the kettle on for a decent cup."

While his mum was putting on her shoes, Charlie looked at Mary-Lou. He had never seen her so quiet. She looked hot and her eyes were puffy as if she'd been crying. It did something funny to Charlie's stomach.

"Shall we take Googoo?" he asked.

She lifted her hand feebly and dropped it again. So Charlie tucked the yellow duck beside her and wheeled the pushchair towards the door. He forgot all about Mrs Tyrer and Guy and the Victoria Cross. He even forgot about the boy in the factory yard.

It was the next morning before he thought of any of them again.

Mary-Lou had been taken from the surgery to the hospital. Mum had gone with her in the ambulance and Charlie had waited for his dad in the surgery. It was the longest thirty minutes of his life. He kept having to grit his teeth so that he didn't cry. What if she died? What if Mary-Lou died? Babies shouldn't die, but he knew they did sometimes. It was so unfair. Perhaps that's what angels were, babies who had died and gone to Heaven. But Mary-Lou was no angel, and Charlie didn't want her to be.

Then the lady in the reception asked him if he wanted a drink or a biscuit or something. He hadn't had any tea yet, but he felt sick and couldn't eat a thing.

He had never thought about God much. Mum and Dad didn't go to church. They never talked about that sort of thing. So he supposed he had no right to speak to someone he had ignored all his life. Perhaps, he thought, if I make a bargain and promise to be a good person, not like Gavin Smedley, then God will make Mary-Lou better. "I will be good," he said to himself. "I will. I will. I'll do my homework and help mum and not ask for a bike."

Then his dad arrived and the lady in reception told him what was happening and that hospital was just a precaution. She was sure that Mary-Lou was going to be fine. How? thought Charlie. How can she know that?

In the hospital waiting room, they waited and waited. It was like sitting in a bubble, cut off from the rest of the world.

"I'll always keep my room tidy," whispered Charlie, "and help mum without moaning, and work hard at school and not ask for things they can't afford."

"What?" said his dad absentmindedly.

"Nothing. I was just ..."

"Praying. I know. Me too."

"About that mountain bike, dad. It doesn't matter. We haven't got any mountains, have we? It'd be daft."

"There's always mountains, Charlie. We just have to go find them."

Christmas. How could they have Christmas without Mary-Lou?

"Dad, is she ...?"

"No, Son. She's going to be fine." And his dad put an arm around his shoulders and squeezed.

Then Mum was coming towards them and she was crying. For one terrible, terrifying moment Charlie felt as though his world had exploded and he'd been blown out into space. But there was a doctor with Mum and when Charlie's feet hit the floor again he realised that the doctor was talking to his dad, telling him that Mary-Lou really was going to be fine. She had an infection or something and they had put her on a drip and she was having antibiotics and was asleep now, but they would be keeping her in for a few days. She was going to be OK. She was going to be OK. Charlie almost fainted with relief. "Thank you, God," he whispered. "Thank you, thank you, thank you." Then he wobbled and almost fell over.

"You've had nothing to eat," said his mum in ashaky voice. "Let's go home and get some tea. I'll come back first thing in the morning. Mary-Lou's in good hands and she's got Googoo to keep her company."

They walked home together. Charlie's mum and dad held hands tightly and Charlie's dad kept one arm around Charlie's shoulders. They hardly said a word, all afraid to speak their fear to each other. *What if ...?* was the question that filled Charlie's head. *What if? What if?* It was too awful to think about.

Yet he couldn't stop thinking it. Two years ago, there'd been no Mary-Lou, but now he couldn't imagine a world without her.

"What can I buy Mary-Lou for Christmas?" he said as they passed a bright store that sent its sparkle out into the street like an invitation.

"We'll think of something nice," said his mum. "Something really special."

At nine-thirty on Saturday morning, there was a knock on the door. Mum's hand went to her heart. It was strange how different knocks could be. This one was urgent, not to be kept waiting.

"I'll go," said Charlie's dad, frowning. "But it's probably someone for our Charlie."

He was right, but it wasn't one of Charlie's friends. It was a policeman – and a policewoman."

"Morning, Sir."

Before he could say anything more Charlie's mum was at the door, almost fainting with fear.

"What's wrong? Is it Mary-Lou?"

"I don't believe that's her name, Madam. It's Edith. Edith Tyrer. Lives at Number Two."

Now Charlie was at the door, all ears, his heart pounding.

"Are you Charlie Pringle?" Charlie nodded, dumbly.

68

The policeman looked at Charlie's dad.

"Can we come in, Sir?"

"Yes, but what's this about? Our little girl's in hospital, you see. We thought ..."

"Ah. Sorry, Sir. No, this is about the old lady at Number Two. She was found in a sad state this morning by the carer, the lady who checks up on her and does her shopping. Seems like someone was there last night. Place is in a bit of a mess and it's come to our attention that young Charlie here has become a regular visitor. One of the neighbours has seen him going there – and the carer knew. Seems the old lady had been telling her about her new friend. We thought he might be able to help us."

Charlie couldn't believe what he was hearing.

Then his dad stood aside and his mum directed them to the living room.

"Now then, young man, when did you last see Mrs Tyrer?"

"The day before yesterday."

The words stuck in his throat.

"And yesterday?"

"I couldn't go yesterday." He looked at his mum and dad. "We were at the hospital because Mary-Lou was sick. I was supposed to go because she was going to tell me about the Victoria Cross. She's got one, you see, and we're doing about the war at school. And she makes a cup of tea and we have biscuits. And she was going to tell me about the ghost, you know, the one in the factory."

Charlie's hand found its way into his pocket and his fingers closed around the tiny wooden mouse. His mum and dad threw puzzled looks at each other.

"OK. Slow down. So you were with your mum and dad last night?"

Charlie nodded. So did his parents.

"Did you come straight home from school?"

Charlie nodded again. Then it seemed as though his stomach turned right over. He thought he was going to be sick and dashed for the sink. The policeman raised his eyebrows and looked at Charlie's dad.

"I was supposed to go at half past four," said Charlie from the sink, "and last time I went there, she didn't check first. She took the chain off and just opened the door."

"Does anyone else go there?"

"Like who?"

"Other kids?"

"I don't think so. No. She said she hasn't talked so much for ages."

"Do any of your mates know about your visits?"

"No!" Then Charlie nodded miserably, remembering how he had wanted to be one up on Stephen. "Yes. Everyone in the class knows, and they know about the medals because I bragged about them, just like Stephen Cropper."

"Medals?"

"Yes, valuable ones. She'd got them all out on the table with the photographs and the carnation and everything."

"We didn't see any medals," said the policeman.

70

"No, that was on Monday. She'd put them away again on Thursday because she'd never told anyone about Guy, and I'm not sure if she wanted to. It was sort of private, you see. Only now she was going to tell me, so I'd have a good story for school.

Is she going to be OK?"

The policeman shrugged. "Hard to say. She's not a young woman. It's the shock as much as anything. That's what does for old folk."

"She's tough," said Charlie. "She does all her own cooking and everything."

"Independent," added his mum, "or so I've heard. They've tried to persuade her to go into a home, but she won't go."

"We don't think she was beaten or anything," said the policewoman, "only knocked over. She hit her head. She's still unconscious."

"Who's this Guy?" asked the policeman.

"Someone Mrs Tyrer knew when she was young. I think he was her boyfriend. He was a hero."

"Did they steal anything?" asked his dad.

"Hard to say. They were looking for something, certainly."

"Can we go to see her?"

"I don't think that would be wise, not yet. We have a few things to clear up."

"But we're friends," said Charlie.

"Hm!" said the policeman, frowning at him. "And what about your other friends? How do you feel about them? Do you think they could have done this?"

Charlie looked at his mum and dad for help. But they looked as bewildered as he felt.

71

"OK," said the policeman, "just one more question. Have you had a fight with anyone, an argument? Has anyone got it in for you?"

"Why do you say that?" asked Charlie's dad.

"Because on the old lady's table was a piece of paper with your name on. It said, 'Charlie Pringle was here'."

"How stupid is that?" said his dad.

"Kids," said the policeman. "Whoever it was, he's not the sharpest pencil in the box. Any ideas?"

"It's probably my piece of paper anyway," said Charlie. "I always write my name on the top, but I didn't write the story down. I was so busy listening, and I can't write fast enough. So I do it when I come home."

He looked at his dad, wondering if he would say anything about Gavin and his record as a troublemaker. But his dad was leaving it to him. No, thought Charlie, *I shouldn't jump to conclusions. I'm going to find out something first.*

"Right. Well, if you think of anything, here's the number to ring. She's at the Royal if you want to enquire about how she's getting on."

"So's our little girl," said Charlie's mum. "We were just getting ready to go in."

"I hope she'll soon be better," said the policewoman.

"It's to be hoped they'll both soon be better," added the policeman grimly. "Otherwise we're looking at something a little more serious."

When they'd gone, Charlie's mum flopped into a chair, and then jumped to her feet again when she thought about Mary-Lou.

"Steady on," said his dad. "Let's have a cup of tea first, before we go to the hospital. Five minutes won't make any difference. Put the kettle on, Charlie, while I phone up to see how the little scamp is doing."

Charlie kept looking at his dad, waiting for him to say something. No one in his class would do such a thing, he was sure of it. But Tim's brother was Gavin Smedley, and he was capable of anything. What if Tim had told him about Mrs Tyrer? He was a bad lot, everyone said, and he'd seen Charlie's dad talking to a policeman. Perhaps he was trying to get Charlie in trouble, just to get his own back. But Charlie's dad hadn't said anything.

****

At the hospital, his mum and dad had to put on gowns and hats and masks before they could go in to see Mary-Lou. Charlie had to be content with waving to her through a window. But she looked much better, and was laughing at him pulling faces at her.

"You'll scare her, dressed like that," he told his mum and dad.

"She'll be all right when she hears our voices," said his mum, "but I won't be able to give her a hug, will I?" And Charlie thought she was going to cry again.

"Perhaps by tomorrow you can," he said.

After a while his dad came out.

"Let's get a drink," he said.

While they were sipping tea and coke he said to Charlie, "Well, do you think it's him?"

"Who?"

"You know who, Gavin Smedley."

73

"It could be anyone."

"True. But I don't think it is, do you? Too much of a coincidence. I wish you'd told us about this medal business."

"Sorry. It was sort of a secret."

"But you told the other kids."

"I didn't mean to. It just came out."

"Has this got anything to do with Stephen beating you at everything?"

"No – yes, I suppose so."

"So what do we do? Do we tell them what happened yesterday in the precinct so they know what kind of a boy he is?"

Charlie shrugged. "He was there on Thursday, outside Mrs Tyrer's. He hit a football against the window and he saw me there, and Tim and Stephen know I go there and about the medals. Wesley said they're worth a lot of money."

"They can be – to someone who collects them. But they're worth far more to the families who treasure them – people like Mrs Tyrer. Is that what he was after, do you think?"

"I don't know."

"But you think it's your fault, don't you?"

Charlie nodded miserably.

"So, do we tell the police?"

"No, not yet. I'll go and see Stephen and Tim. Perhaps they know what happened."

"Do you think that's a good idea?"

"They're my friends."

"OK. But just go to their houses. If they're not there, don't go looking for them. Come straight home. Understand?"

"OK. Can we find out how Mrs Tyrer is now?"

"Are you relatives," the nurse asked.

"No," said Charlie's dad. "Just friends. Well, neighbours really. I don't think she's got any family."

"Then you can't see her, I'm afraid. She's in a private room with a policewoman, but she has regained consciousness, I can tell you that."

"Has she said anything?" asked Charlie.

The nurse frowned. "I'm not at liberty to say. Policeman's orders," she said importantly. "Now, if you'll excuse me, we are rather short-staffed."

****

Charlie left his dad at the corner of Finchley Street. His mum was coming home later. He walked to Tim's house first. Tim lived in a red brick terrace. They were quite big houses with bay windows and tiny gardens in the front. He knocked on the door and Tim's mum answered, wiping her hands on a tea towel.

"Hello, Charlie. Tim's not here. He's gone into town with his dad to look for some football boots. Then they're going to the match."

"Oh!"

"Was it important?"

Charlie nodded. "Is Gavin in?"

"Still in bed, lazy little sod. I'll shout him if you like, but I warn you he's not in the best of moods when he wakes up."

He would go and see Stephen, just to talk to him, see if he knew anything. Sometimes he hung around with Gavin, when there was no one else to play with. It was a bit of a walk to Stephen's part of town. The pavements were wider and there were trees. *It's nice*, thought Charlie. *I'd like to live here.*

He walked up the drive and lifted his hand to press the bell, but his hand stopped in mid-air. Someone was yelling. Someone else was yelling back, almost screaming, hysterical, mum would say. He listened hard, but couldn't hear a voice that sounded like Stephen's. He waited for the shouting to stop but it didn't. He turned to go, then heard something crash to the floor and saw someone through the coloured glass door in the hall, dashing towards him. The door was yanked open and Stephen's dad burst out, pulling on an overcoat as he strode down the steps. He stopped when he saw Charlie.

"What do you want?" he asked, without smiling.

"Is Stephen in?"

"No, Stephen isn't in, and you wouldn't like to be in his shoes when he is. You obviously don't *know* where he is?"

"No."

Mr Cropper got into his car, slammed it into gear and flew out of the drive. As the wheels spun, they sprayed gravel over the flowerbeds – and Charlie.

He knocked on the open door.

Mrs Cropper didn't come.

"Who is it?" a voice came from the back somewhere.

"Charlie Pringle."

"What do you want, Charlie?"

"I wanted Stephen, but he's not here, is he?"

Stephen's mum appeared at the end of the wide hallway. At least, Charlie *thought* it was her. She usually had lots of makeup on – and posh clothes. She looked different, sort of grey and old.

"Come in, Charlie."

He went in and closed the door. In the kitchen, he stepped carefully over the broken china and stood, feeling uncomfortable. He'd never heard his own mum and dad fighting.

"Accident," she said, pointing at the mess.

"Clumsy me."

She lit a cigarette and sat down at the table. Then she looked at Charlie and stubbed it out. "Stephen's disappeared," she said. "I thought he was in bed. I didn't see him last night. I don't always. I was out, you see. And this morning – well he wasn't there and his bed hasn't been slept in."

"Where would he go?"

"How should I know? I don't know what he does, who his friends are – except you of course. And you're a sensible boy aren't you, Charlie. He's very grown-up is Stephen, looks after himself, always has. He likes being independent. Doesn't want a mother who fusses. Does your mother fuss?"

Charlie shrugged. He didn't think 'fuss' was quite the right word.

"Perhaps he's gone to his granddad's."

"He'd have a job. One granddad lives in Canada and the other one's in Aberdeen."

"Which one was in the RAF?"

Mrs Cropper shook her head. "That's a laugh. Have you seen the pair of them? They both did National Service for two years, but that's about all."

"Were they in the war?"

"Not old enough."

"So whose are the medals?"

"What medals? What on earth are you talking about?"

"Has Stephen told you what we're doing at school about the war and stuff?"

She lifted her shoulders and shook her head. "He just gets on with it. I don't ask. Never liked schoolwork much. Look, unless you know where Stephen is you might as well go. What's he playing at, that's what I'd like to know. Give him everything, we do, and this is the thanks we get – and who gets the blame for it? Me, that's who. As if I haven't got enough on my plate."

"Do you think I could see Stephen's bedroom?"

"I don't know. Why? What do you want? Are you playing at being a detective?"

"I'm not sure, but perhaps there'll be a clue or something. Have you phoned the police?"

"Of course we've phoned the police."

"Is that where Mr Cropper's gone?"

"No, Mr Cropper's gone to work," she frowned.

"You ask a lot of questions. OK then, but be quick. You can look, but better not touch anything. They'll be here any minute."

Charlie went upstairs. Mrs Cropper didn't bother to go with him.

One look around Stephen's room told Charlie that Stephen did have everything, if music systems and TVs and computers were everything. Suddenly, Charlie knew that they weren't and that he wouldn't really want to change places with Stephen.

He felt like a thief, an intruder, afraid to touch anything, anyway, in case it gave him away. He wouldn't want Stephen to know he'd been here. He stood rooted to the spot and just looked. When his eyes came to rest on the desk, he saw Stephen's homework book, and beside it another book, old, with a faded blue cover. He walked over to the desk and looked at the book. It was called, 'They'll Never Give Up' and had been written in 1941. It lay open on page sixty-five. He turned it over quickly, glanced down the pages and then read, from the top:

It seems that Wilson was on patrol over Southampton in a Hurricane, and decided to chase a Junkers. Instead, he found himself in front of a Messerschmitt 110 which proceeded to pour cannon shells into his plane. What happened after that is described in the official account as follows:

One shell tore through the hood and sent splinters into his right eye. The second shell struck his spare petrol tank, which exploded and set the machine on fire. The third shell crashed into the cockpit and tore away his trouser leg. The fourth hit his left foot and took off some of his toes.

"Blimey!" said Charlie.

As Flight-Lieutenant Wilson turned to avoid further shots into his burning plane he suddenly found the Messerschmitt had overtaken him and was right on his gun-sight. His dashboard was shattered and was, in his own words, 'dripping like wax with the heat.' The Messerschmitt was 200 yards in front.

As Flight-Lieutenant Wilson pressed the gun button, he could see one of the fingers on his right-hand blistering in the heat. He could also see his left hand, which was holding the throttle open, blistering in the flames.

The Messerschmitt zigzagged this way and that, trying to avoid the hail of fire from the blazing Hurricane. By this time the heat was so great that Wilson had to put his feet on the seat beneath his parachute.

He continued the fight for several minutes until the Messerschmitt disappeared in a steep dive. Eyewitnesses later reported they had seen it crash a few miles out to sea.

On losing sight of the enemy, Wilson attempted to jump out, but struck his head on the hood above him. He immediately threw back the hood and tried to jump again.

Then he realised he had not undone the strap holding him in the cockpit. One of these straps broke. He undid the other, and then at last succeeded in jumping.

He dived headfirst and after several somersaults in the air he pulled the rip-cord with considerable difficulty. It took him something like twenty minutes to reach the ground.

A Messerschmitt came screaming past, and as he floated down he pretended he was dead. When the Messerschmitt had gone he noticed for the first time that his left heel had been struck.

Blood was oozing out of the lace-holes of his boots. He tried to see what other injuries he had received, and found that he was able to move all his limbs.

At one moment as he was coming down he thought he would hit a high-tension cable, but managed to manoeuvre in the sky so that he missed it. Reaching the ground he saw a cyclist and managed to land in a field near to him.

While he was landing, with sixty pieces of metal in him, Wilson was shot once more – this time by an inexperienced member of the Home Guard. The first thing he did when they got him to a hospital was send a wire to his fiancée, a Red Cross Nurse.

Shot down, Darling. Very slightly hurt ... All my love ...

Charlie looked up quickly. Someone was knocking on the door, demanding attention. Another policeman's knock. But he couldn't resist a whistle. "Now that's what I call a hero," he said to himself.

There was no need to look at Stephen's homework book. The stories were almost identical, except for the fact that Stephen had put some of it into his own words and couldn't resist adding bits to make it even more exciting. Instead of Wilson, of course, Stephen's hero was called 'Cropper'.

Didn't he know that names were written on medals? Well, if he hadn't known before, chances are he would know now, if he'd bothered to look, because suddenly, Charlie was sure that it was Stephen who had paid Mrs Tyrer a visit. He hadn't got the medals he'd bragged about so he thought he'd borrow some.

Who'd have thought it? Not rotten Gavin Smedley, but Stephen Cropper, his friend since he was five. It all made Charlie feel a bit sick. I mean, you think you know people, don't you? You think you understand how things are in the world around you. Then something happens to turn everything on its head and you don't know anything anymore.

Stephen was his friend, wasn't he? How could he do this? How could he walk away and leave old Mrs Tyrer lying unconscious? Suddenly, Charlie didn't care where Stephen was. He deserved to be cold and frightened and lost. Charlie wouldn't help to look for him. Charlie would go home and start making something to cheer up Mrs Tyrer.

He tiptoed downstairs.

"Bye, Mrs Cropper," he said, too softly for her and the policeman to hear.

He walked home slowly.

He was angry with Stephen – and disappointed, but at the same time he couldn't stop himself thinking about Mr Cropper going to work when his only son had disappeared – and about Mrs Cropper not knowing who Stephen's friends were or if he had homework. Charlie's parents weren't like that. They knew where he was and who he was with every minute of the day and if they couldn't help him with his homework, they made sure the help came from somewhere. They loved him, and he knew that every minute of every day. It wasn't true that they loved Mary-Lou more. Her needs were different, that was all. She was still a baby. But Stephen Cropper had wanted Charlie to feel the same way he did – unloved, uncared about, like a piece of furniture they'd grown tired of. Why did he want to do that? Could it be that he was envious of Charlie, when all the time Charlie thought it was the other way around?

Poor Stephen.

Where could he have gone?

What if Stephen thought Mrs Tyrer was dead?

Charlie thought about all the places they'd played. Where was there anywhere to hide? He thought about the park and the waste ground at the end of Jermyn Street. But there was nowhere you could shelter from the cold and stay hidden.

He thought about it all through lunch. Dad made him beans on toast and Charlie made the tea. Then someone knocked on the door. It was the policeman. They both knew it instinctively and looked at each other. It seemed an age before Charlie's dad went to let him in.

"How's the little girl, Mr Pringle?"

"Better, thank you. The wife's with her now. I'm going down again later."

"Glad to hear it. The old lady's better, too. You were right. She is a tough old nut. We've put a few questions to her but she keeps saying the same thing over and over."

"What's that, then?" asked Charlie's dad. "Does she know who her visitors were?"

"We haven't pressed her yet. She's still very weak. But she keeps saying, 'Charlie Pringle sent them'."

Charlie almost choked on his toast.

"But I didn't! Dad, I didn't! I know I shouldn't have told them about Mrs Tyrer and the medals and everything, but I never thought anyone would do this."

"It's a sad world sometimes," said the policeman.

"You can't be too careful, you know."

Charlie had to turn away. Boys didn't cry.

"It's OK, Son," said the policeman. "You see, she's still rather confused. She could just be repeating what they said to her. It would be a way of getting her to let them in if they knew she trusted you.

84

"And, given some peace and quiet, she'll soon be able to give us a description, I hope. Then, we'll get this mess sorted in good time for Christmas. It might just be some sort of joke gone wrong. You got any more ideas yourself, young Charlie?"

"You said 'them'. So it wasn't just one?"

"Apparently not." Charlie shook his head.

"You're absolutely sure it's kids then?" said his dad.

"No doubt about it. Footprints on the linoleum. Kids' trainers. And a couple of bubble-gum wrappers. Don't quite see Mrs Tyrer as a gum-chewer. We'll get 'em Sir, don't you fret."

There was a sharp noise coming from his pocket.

"'Scuse me. Doubleday here. Go ahead."

He walked from the room, but was only gone a minute.

"Seems one of your young pals has gone missing."

Charlie nodded.

"You knew?" said his dad.

Charlie nodded again. "Stephen."

"Stephen Cropper?"

"Uh-huh. I went there, didn't I, and his mum and dad were having a row about him because he'd gone. They should have been worried but they were just angry."

"Is he your best pal?" asked the policeman.

"He was," said Charlie, "but he's not now, not if he's got anything to do with this."

"You think he was at Mrs Tyrer's?"

Charlie shrugged. "He might have been."

"Any ideas where he might have gone?"

"No. I've been trying to think, but I don't know."

"Well, if you have any bright ideas you know where to find us."

****

85

When the policeman had gone, Charlie's dad set off for the hospital. Charlie asked him to please buy some freesias for Mrs Tyrer and to say they were from Charlie Pringle and that he was sorry.

"Why don't you come with me?"

"I have to stay here and think. I'll be all right, Dad."

"OK. I won't be long, anyway. I'll just see if your mum and Mary-Lou are all right and if they need anything."

Charlie went to his room and knelt on the chair by the window. He looked down at the canal, wondering where the water went, if it went anywhere. It didn't seem to be moving at all, not like a river. It must be nice to live by a river where the water is clear and you can see to the bottom and there are swans and ducks and kingfishers maybe – and fish of course. His eyes strayed across to the high fence and the dark, empty shell of the shoe factory. He'd always imagined it was full of ghosts, and at night, when everyone slept, he imagined the factory came alive. The stitching machines whirred and tapped, young boys ran about on errands and the barges pulled slowly up and down the canal. When he woke up, he often imagined he could smell the freshly tanned leather – which was strange when he didn't really know what it smelt like.

His eyes followed the fence as far as he could see it along the other side of the canal. The boardings were blackened and some of them were broken. Perhaps some of the fence was, too, somewhere he couldn't see from the window, just enough for a boy to get through. But Stephen would never go there, surely. It was a dangerous place. They'd always been warned about it, and Stephen was too sensible.

86

He was right about the fence – there must be a way in – because he could see a boy standing in the yard. It was daylight so it wasn't just a shadow in the moonlight but a real boy. Stephen? No. Charlie could see his clothes, his face, and he wasn't an ordinary boy. He had short trousers on and long socks up to his knees. He wore a scarf around his neck and a cap and jacket like old men sometimes wore. And he was looking straight at Charlie. Then he lifted his arm and beckoned urgently. *Perhaps, somehow, he knows where Stephen is.*

Charlie put his hand in his pocket for a tissue, something white to wave. He wondered if the boy could see him at all. But the boy had turned away, and all Charlie found in his pocket was the tiny, wooden mouse.

"I'm coming!" shouted Charlie, though the window was closed. "I'm coming! Wait for me!"

AND THAT'S WHEN THINGS GOT REALLY WEIRD.

To start with, it was going dark too early, even for December. He grabbed his coat and ran from his room, out into the hall and through the door, pulling it shut behind him. He flew down the stairs two at a time and out through the big door at the bottom. Around the side of the flats he went and down a flight of steps to the towpath. He followed the canal to a footbridge and crossed over. That's when the smell reached him.

No, it wasn't the smell of leather or the smoke from coal fires, but it was smoke. Charlie ran along the high fence.

Dirty grey weeds grew along it, but instead of the crimson of coke cans and cornflower blue of crisp packets, there was the odd clump of tall daisies and rosebay willowherb. Someone had cleared away the supermarket carrier bags that were always snagged on the broken wires, and a dumped trolley, full of empty bottles, had disappeared. Charlie kicked at the fence, searching for a way in, but the fence was solid and there didn't seem to be any gaps. Stephen couldn't be here anyway, could he? He simply wasn't that stupid. Charlie wondered if he should have phoned the police or the fire brigade first, but he hadn't noticed the smoke then. Suddenly, he realised the smell of burning was everywhere. It wasn't coming from the factory as he had thought, but from the whole town.

When he looked back, he could see that the streetlights had been switched off, there were no car headlights and no yellow glow from any window. It seemed the whole world had been blacked out except for, here and there, a crimson glow that rose into the sky. And there was a noise unlike any that Charlie had ever heard before, except in films. It was the throb and drone of aeroplanes, not jets flying to sunny places, or even Tornadoes on training flights, but World War Two bombers flying low over the town, humming like terrible bees.

Charlie began to shake. He pinched himself to make sure he was awake.

Then he heard a shrill, whining sound followed by a roar and a thud. Then more whining and droning and thudding until his head felt as if it were bursting.

88

"Stephen," he kept telling himself, trying to focus on what was real. "I must find Stephen. He must be in the factory – and they're dropping bombs. We have to get to an air raid shelter." But that was a crazy thought. There weren't any air raid shelters now, were there?

Briefly, he wondered about his mum and dad and Mary-Lou and the hospital. The thought made his head spin. Were they safe, or were they part of another dream?

He was still looking for a way into the yard when he saw the boy standing outside the main gate, beckoning again.

The gate was open – but it hadn't been open for years! It hadn't looked as if it *would* open any more. Charlie ran back along the towpath just in time to see the boy disappearing down the road.

"Wait!" he shouted. "Don't go so fast!"

The boy stopped, looked back briefly at him and carried on running.

Charlie gave a spurt, trying to catch up with him, when he saw a man coming towards him from around a corner. He was wearing a long coat and a steel hat. He was carrying a torch with a kind of hood on it and across his chest a bag was strapped. "Ere!" he shouted. "Where you off to then? Your nearest shelter's under the co-op on Jermyn Street. Where's your ma and pa?"

Charlie pointed after the boy.

"I have to get my brother," he said. "He's run off."

"Where'd you come from then?"

Charlie pointed back. "Priory Gardens."

"Priory what? You mean Priory Road that was flattened last week. Where you living now, then?"

Charlie couldn't answer him. He was gaping in astonishment. Where Priory Gardens had stood, there was the remains of a row of houses. Doors were blown out and roofs caved in. He could see an iron bedstead hanging from what was left of the upstairs floor.

"What's going on?" he said, touching the man's coat to make sure it was real.

"You shell-shocked or sum'ing?" asked the Warden. "The bleedin' Blitz is going on, that's what. Where you been the last two months? Now get along into a shelter. They 'aven't finished with us yet. An' where's your mask? You 'aven't got no mask. What you playin' at then?"

"It's at home," said Charlie. "I forgot it."

"An' now it's been blown up, I suppose." He opened his bag and pulled something out. "'ere, 'ave this one. It's not a Mickey Mouse one, but I always carry a spare in case I meets a daft blighter like you. You're old enough t'know better, y'know that. It might be a bit on the big side, but it's better than nothing an' I can probably get another. I don't know you, do I, an' I know most of the kids down Priory Street. What number you from?"

"Number Twenty-Six."

"This is no time to be takin' the mickey. You're askin' for a clip round the ear, you are. They only goes up to twenty. I knows that for a fact."

"Yes, Sir. We haven't lived there long. It must be Number Sixteen."

"Hm! Well, you'd better get along then, sharpish.

It's going t'be a long night. Your ma'll be looking for you. Best just give me your name then, Son, for my report, like."

"It's Charlie Pringle – and I don't belong here. I'm going to wake up in a moment."

"That's what we all say, Son. That's what we all say. Get along now, while there's a bit of quiet."

Charlie was having a nightmare. He was certain of it. He tried walking with his eyes closed, hoping he would wake up, but it was impossible as well as dangerous. The smell made his nostrils smart and there was choking dust in the air.

He opened his eyes again and coughed. Where on earth was he?

He should be at the end of Burnham Road, near the new industrial estate, but this was nothing like the town he knew. He was passing a cinema. It was closed and there were no lights on but he could just about read the sign, 'THE GAUMONT'.

He bit his lip and pinched his arm, but nothing would make him wake up. Then he thought of the boy. Where had he gone? Why hadn't he waited? Without him, Charlie had no idea where he was going or where he would be safe. If he turned around now and headed back, would everything return to normal? Would Priory Gardens be there instead of a smoking ruin?

He stopped outside a fish and chip shop. There were boards across the window and a sign that said, 'FRYING TONIGHT' with a line through it. Underneath it, someone had written, 'OR TOMORROW IF THE BLEEDIN' GERMANS WILL LET US. TO 'ELL WITH 'ITLER.'

Charlie turned around. What could he do but go back? He didn't belong here. This was Mrs Tyrer's time. He wondered for a moment where she was and what she was doing in her sparkling white apron and with her smile to match. Somehow, he felt that all this was down to her and her stories. Just going into her flat was like stepping back in time, as if she lived in the past and couldn't let go of it.

But he couldn't go back yet, he knew that, not until he found out why he was here. He looked down the dark street. Through the smoke and dust, he saw a pale moon, and beneath it, standing on a heap of bricks, was the grey silhouette of the boy.

The moment Charlie spotted him, the boy moved on and Charlie set off after him again. An eerie silence had settled over everywhere now the planes had gone. Fires were burning, but none close to him, though buildings smouldered and dust rose from those newly demolished. Occasionally, looking down, Charlie saw a crack of light at a basement window. And from far away an angry voice, *the warden's,* he thought, telling someone to turn off a light. Otherwise, the town seemed empty of any life, till a cat broke from the shadows and streaked across his path. Charlie felt it brush his leg before it disappeared down some steps. Well, that was real enough.

His heart was thumping. In that moment, when he'd turned to look at the cat, the boy had disappeared again.

Charlie walked on slowly, his hand over his mouth to keep out the dust, which seemed to be getting thicker and thicker until he felt he couldn't breathe. He stopped again. There was rubble all over the road now so he had to feel his way carefully. A building on his left must have been recently hit – or shaken to its foundations by near miss. He could hear bricks falling and timbers cracking. His eyes had grown more accustomed to the poor light, and in the clouds of dust he saw the boy again. He was walking into the ruin where ragged walls were leaning and the roof was caving in.

"You can't go in there!" Charlie yelled. "Come away from it! It's falling down!"

But the boy didn't seem to hear him. He stepped further into the rubble and disappeared.

Charlie looked around him. He heard a bell clanging and prayed it was a fire engine coming his way, but the sound grew less and the fire engine turned down another street. He looked around, hoping to see someone who could help, but there was no one. Just him, Charlie Pringle, standing in the dust and darkness and silence of a town after the bombs have fallen. Silent, that is, except for the distant wailing of sirens and voices that seemed to come from the other side of sleep. Then he heard a cry, a single heart-rending cry of, "Mummy!" It was a baby's cry, a girl, he thought, and at first he couldn't tell where it was coming from. It seemed to come from the sky.

Mary-Lou! he thought in confusion. *Mary-Lou!*
But how could it be?
He listened, concentrating.
"Mummy!"
The cry was coming from the fallen house.
But Mary-Lou was in the hospital.
There it was again.
Charlie moved nearer to the crumbling house.

"Is anyone there?" If the boy was there, why didn't he answer?

Why did they bomb houses with children in? wondered Charlie angrily. Children couldn't fight wars. He remembered Mary-Lou's face laughing at him in the hospital and his mum's tears of relief when she knew Mary-Lou was going to be OK.

"Mummy!"

He waited and watched as a few seconds ticked painfully away. The bricks had stopped falling – for the moment at least, but when Charlie dared to look up, he saw the pale plaster of a chimney breast outlined against the darkness, waiting to come crashing down.

Slowly, carefully, sometimes dropping to his hands and knees, he followed the way the boy had taken into the house. He could see a doorframe but no wall, and pitch darkness beyond. He moved carefully, painfully slowly, glancing up and all around, aware that everything was shifting, disintegrating around him. But he couldn't get through the low doorway. The ceiling had fallen in. Everything was such a mess. He felt around. There were pieces of wood, a staircase possibly, and all of it seemed to have collapsed into the tiny space behind the door.

Charlie tried to lift the splinters of wood and lumps of plaster, brick and tile, straining to see, wishing he had a torch. Then he heard the cry again. Slowly, very slowly, one piece at a time Charlie edged away the rubble, terrified that one wrong move would bring everything tumbling in on him and the baby – until there was a space large enough to crawl through. He reached out his hand and felt about him. Oh, if only he could see! His fingers touched a tiny hand. It was warm. Small fingers wrapped themselves around his thumb and the baby whimpered.

"It's OK," he said, with a confidence he didn't feel. "I'm going to get you out."

But where was the boy? Where could he have gone?

Charlie tried to turn around in the tiny space, but it was difficult and he scraped his knee. He felt about him and yelled out loud when his hand touched a bare, cold leg.

"Billy," said the baby. "Billy."

Charlie swallowed hard. He had to be sure. He gasped when his fingers found an arm in the sleeve of a jacket. They moved up and touched a neck that was cold and wet, and a torn shirt. When his fingers moved down, they found a single button held by a thread, and braces pulled apart. He found the arm again, the wrist, the hand. Their fingers touched.

His own were cold but the hand he squeezed was colder. It was the boy. He was sure of it. He drew away sharply, and winced when something sharp caught his hand. He felt around carefully so that whatever it was wouldn't harm the baby. Beside the body, he found what felt like a small penknife.

He wiped the dust from it, folded it safely and shoved it in his pocket.

"Billy!" said the baby again. "Alice want Billy."

But Billy was dead.

Charlie swallowed a lump in his throat. "Hello, Alice," he whispered.

"Billy," said the baby. "Billy. Alice wants Mummy."

"I'm not Billy," he said. "I'm Charlie."

Charlie wondered if she was injured, but her arms and legs felt OK and there was no time to wait for someone else to come. He turned her around as gently as he could and began pulling her backwards through the hole.

She was crying now, whimpering softly, like Mary-Lou did sometimes in her sleep. So Charlie kept talking to her, wondering where her mother was, hoping she wasn't dead like Billy.

When they were both back through the hole, Charlie picked up the little girl.

"Foo-Foo!" she said, straining in his arms.

"What?"

"Foo-Foo!" and Charlie almost dropped her as she squirmed after something in the rubble. He crouched down and felt around quickly until his hand touched something soft. It was a rag doll. He shook off the dust and crumbs of plaster and gave it to her. The little girl clasped it tightly and Charlie made his way slowly back through the ruin.

As he sat in the middle of the road, Charlie had no idea of time, but while he sat, the chimney crashed down and the doorframe, through which he had crawled, disappeared. He sat as far away from buildings and falling masonry as he could, rocking the little girl in his arms.

97

She clung to him with one arm and to her rag-doll with the other, hardly making a sound. When she did whimper and begin to cry again, Charlie remembered the wooden mouse. He took it from his pocket and pressed it into her hand. He knew how warm and comforting the wood felt.

"Billy's mouse," she said, and was quiet.

When Charlie was numb with cold and thought he would be sitting there forever until he became frozen in time like those people in Pompey, he was aware of voices without bodies moving towards him through the smoky air. Then, in a ghostly procession, the bodies followed. He heard a woman's voice, hysterical, and a man's, calm, trying to placate her. She was screaming now, crying out when she saw the house. "Half an hour, that's all I meant to be. I 'ad to see if Gran was OK so I left them under the stairs. Billy's a good boy, a sensible boy. We were going down the shelter but there was no time. I should never have left them. Billy! Billy!"

Charlie struggled to get up with the baby still in his arms. Until then no one had seen his grey shape among the rubble on the street.

"'ere, what's this then?" said one of the men.

"Is this your boy, Missis?"

The woman stumbled back from the debris of her house, her face alight with hope. "Billy?"

She put out her hands to him, then saw his face and recoiled in shock and disappointment.

"That's not our Billy!"

98

Charlie was sorry he was not Billy. He tried to speak, to tell them Billy was dead, but no words came out. His head was swimming and he knew he was going to faint. As he pushed the little girl towards her mother, his knees buckled and one of the men caught him as he fell.

"Alice! Alice! He's got our Alice!"

They were the last words he heard.

****

"Charlie! Charlie! What a silly sausage, going to sleep in your chair. Come on, now. It's not even teatime.

I hope you're not sickening for something, too."

"No. I can't stay here. Got to go home."

"You are home, you daftie. You must have been dreaming. Come on now love, you'll be getting cold in here. There's no radiator on. Oh, my goodness! You are cold! Come and have a cup of tea. I'll put a drop of your dad's Christmas whisky in. That'll warm you up. What have you been doing? Your hands are filthy. Go and wash them quick before you come for your tea."

Charlie stretched his cramped and aching limbs. Mum was right. His hands were filthy. Good thing she hadn't seen the blood. He stared at his scraped knee. What on earth had he been doing before he fell asleep? He looked through the window. Four o'clock and it was almost dark. His knee was hurting. There was no sign of the moon yet, but in the wash of the town light, he saw a familiar outline in the factory yard. It was Billy. His stomach churned as everything flooded back. This time, the boy was moving towards the factory, and although Charlie couldn't see him clearly, he knew that he was beckoning to him.

"Dad!" he shouted. "Dad!"

"What's the matter? What's wrong?"

His dad came rushing in.

"I think I know where Stephen is and I think he might be in trouble."

"Then we'll phone the police," said his dad.

"No, let's make sure first. It won't take us long. Then we can phone them."

"Well, you are not going anywhere until you've had something to warm you," said his mum, and there was no arguing with her.

"Mrs Tyrer's mother used to put whisky in their tea at Christmas," said Charlie. "I wonder how she is."

"On the mend," said his dad. "The nurse said she's a real fighter. You can go to see her tomorrow, if you like."

After a warming cup of whisky tea and a jam sandwich, Charlie and his dad set off down the towpath and over the bridge. He saw the coke cans and crisp packets and dumped trolley in the light of his dad's torch. He glanced back towards the town to make sure all was still as it should be.

"There must be a way in somewhere," he said. He glanced up and saw Billy, pointing. "Look!"

His dad shone the torch. "Look where?"

Charlie directed the beam of the torch. The yard was empty.

"It's OK. I thought I saw something or someone. I think we've got to look further down, Dad. Come on! We have to hurry."

They had to push their way through a mesh of brambles and clumps of old dock before they found the breach in the fence. It was only small and Charlie's dad had to scrape some of the ground away to make a gap big enough for him to get through.

"Kids must have made it," he said. "I've never seen any kids in here."

With Billy in front of them, waving them on, how could Charlie doubt it?

"I just know he's here," he said. "But we have to find a way in."

"It's all boarded up. It's been like that for years. Do you *really* think this is where he is? Why would he come here? I can't imagine Stephen is mixed up in anything nasty."

"Let's just find him, Dad. Then we'll find out. Look, one of the boards is broken," said Charlie, looking at the spot from where Billy had disappeared.

"Well, I'm blowed if I could tell," said his dad. "You must have better eyes than me, Charlie. Here, I'll give you a leg up. But be careful. We don't want that board crashing down on us now, do we? Just push it aside a bit and shine the torch in. Mind you, I don't think you'll see much. It's a fair size, is that place."

He lifted Charlie up until Charlie could stand on his shoulders.

"What about your back, Dad?"

"Be quick about it, and I'll be OK. If Stephen's in there, we must fetch the police – or the fire brigade."

"Or the ambulance."

Charlie shone the torch. It was like lighting a match in a cave.

"Stephen! Are you in there?"

"No one there but ghosts," said his dad. "I thought Stephen had got more sense. He wouldn't come somewhere like this. Places like this are dangerous.

I don't know why they haven't flattened it before now."

No, Charlie agreed. *Stephen wasn't stupid. But he was here.*

He cupped his hand around his mouth and yelled. "Stephen!"

"Push me up a bit, Dad, and I can get through. You go and get help."

"Charlie? What the heck … Where's Gavin?"

"Not likely," called Charlie's dad, "there'll be a fair drop down the other side."

"No, Dad. There's a kind of bench or something. I can lower myself down on to it. Honest. I can do it. Push me up, Dad, please."

"Your mum'll kill me."

"I won't let her. She knows how stubborn I can be."

Charlie's dad held on to Charlie's ankles and pushed him up until Charlie could squeeze through the broken boarding.

"Watch out for broken glass," his dad warned.

"I can't see any," said Charlie, "but I'll be careful."

He heaved himself through, wondering how Stephen could have got through on his own. If he had help then Charlie had a pretty good idea who it had been.

He shone the torch before lowering himself down to within a foot of the bench. Then he let go of the brick window frame and dropped like a cat.

He switched his torch on again. "Stephen?"

"Charlie? What are you doing here?"

"Are you OK?"

"I'm freezing, and I've hurt my ankle. It might be broken. I can't move it. Did Gavin send you? Have you brought any food? He said he'd come back last night, but he didn't, the moron. This is all his fault."

Charlie took off his anorak and put it around Stephen's shoulders.

"What on earth are you doing here, you idiot?"

"I'm on the run. Don't you know? I killed someone. I didn't mean to. I sort of slipped and bumped into her and she fell and knocked her head. Gavin said she was dead. He said if I hid here they'd think I was dead too. No one ever comes here. Then they'd stop looking for me and I could go away somewhere."

"Don't be stupid! What about your mum and dad? Everyone'll be out looking for you. They're probably dragging the canal right now."

Stephen was silent. Then, "You got anything to eat? I'm starving."

"No," said Charlie. "And Mrs Tyrer's not dead. She could have been for all you cared, but she's not. She's going to be OK. She's tough is Mrs Tyrer."

"You sure? You're not kidding me?"

"Of course I'm sure. I wouldn't lie about something like that, would I?"

Stephen began to cry. Charlie was embarrassed. In six years he had never seen Stephen cry. He shone his torch on the injured ankle. It looked enormous and Stephen had taken his shoe off.

"I tried to climb out," he said. "This place is pretty scary at night. It creaks and groans. You'd think there were ghosts here if you believed in that rubbish. When I fell, I must have hit my head, because I heard someone saying he was going to fetch help, but I would have to wait a while because there was something else he had to do first. I don't remember seeing anyone in the dark, but he said his name was ..."

Suddenly, there were voices outside. Something was being dragged or rolled.

"The oil drum," explained Stephen. "That's how we got in."

"Dad?" shouted Charlie. But it wasn't his dad. It was Gavin Smedley and one of his mates. A light shone down from the broken boarding.

"What do you think you're doing here, Pringle? You're not supposed to be here."

"About time, Smedley," said Stephen. "Where've you been? I'm starving."

"Slept late, didn't I?"

"But it's dark, you moron."

"Here." Gavin threw down a small package.

Charlie caught it and opened it.

It was a peanut butter sandwich.

"I hate peanut butter," moaned Stephen, before biting into it hungrily.

"So what are you doing here, Pringle? Did that prat of a brother of mine tell you where your precious little friend was?"

"I haven't seen Tim," said Charlie. "I worked it out for myself."

"So what are you going to do now? Are you going to blab? I s'pose he's told you everything."

"He didn't have to," said Charlie. "I guessed, about the medals and everything. It was a stupid idea, telling Mrs Tyrer I sent you. You can't steal something like the Victoria Cross. It's got a name on."

"It was just for a laugh!" shouted Gavin.

"Who's laughing?" said Charlie.

"You're such wimp, Pringle. No sense of adventure."

"We weren't going to steal anything," said Stephen. "We just wanted to see it and ask her if we could borrow it for a bit, that's all. But she'd hidden it. Then he offered to help her look for it and when I wouldn't join in, he thumped me – and that's when I slipped and bumped into her. You're a moron, Gavin Smedley. You said she was dead."

"You'll have to own up," said Charlie.

"I know," said Stephen. "I'm sorry, Charlie. It was a rotten thing to do."

"Own up?" yelled down Gavin. "No way. I'm not getting caught. It's his word against mine, anyway. And I've got an alibi. Tim'll swear blind I was in the precinct with him. I just know he will. So long, you two wimps. C'mon Denz." (Denz was one of his mates) "Ouch!"

"Not so fast, young man. You're not going anywhere, not without us, anyway."

Charlie recognised the voice of the policeman.

"The cavalry's arrived," said Charlie.

"What?" said Stephen, who didn't have a Western-mad granddad.

"Help," explained Charlie.

"You OK, Charlie?"

"Hi, Dad. Yes, I'm fine, but Stephen's hurt his ankle and he's really cold. He can't stand up."

The constable's face appeared above them, shining like the moon in his own torchlight, which he then directed down on them. "Hang on, lads, the paramedics are on their way – and the fire brigade. If we need to get a stretcher in there, they'll have to make a better way in. Do you want a Mars bar?"

"Yes, please," said Stephen.

****

At eight o'clock, Charlie was drinking a steaming mug of hot chocolate, thinking about everything that had happened. Was it still only Saturday? He could hardly believe it. So much had happened, things he would remember all his life. He fell asleep watching TV and his dad carried him to bed.

****

On Sunday afternoon, Charlie had three people to visit in the hospital. Mary-Lou was first of course and Charlie was allowed in to see her. He gave her a hug and she pulled his hair.

"I think she's feeling much better," said Charlie to his dad.

His mum and dad smiled at them both.

"She can come home tomorrow," said his mum.

"At this moment, I don't believe I will ever shout at her again, and she can have the moon for Christmas."

"Course you will," said Charlie, "or she'll grow up spoilt."

Then he went to see Mrs Tyrer. She was sitting in an armchair at the side of her bed and was wrapped in a warm, purple shawl.

She smiled when she saw Charlie.

"Hi," he said, not sure what else he was going to say.

"Pull up a chair," said Mrs Tyrer.

Charlie did so and sat down.

"I'm sorry," he said.

"Not your fault."

"I didn't tell them to come and see you. I wouldn't do that."

"I know. It was just a sort of dare, a lark. They didn't really mean any harm."

"But I did tell them about you and the medals and everything. I was bragging because Stephen is always the best at everything and I was sick of it."

"Ah, I see. Do you know what our Tom used to do for a lark? He'd climb up on people's roofs and stuff a lump of turf down the chimney to smoke them out."

Charlie gasped. "That's not funny!"

"No. But he thought so. Used to wait for them to come running out, coughing. Laughed about it for days. Boys will be boys."

"They didn't steal anything, though, did they?"

"No, they wanted to see the medals, but I didn't trust them, especially that one with the spiky hair. Looked like a hedgehog, I thought, only not nearly as sweet," she giggled. "They were in the bread bin – the medals. Probably still are. Don't ask me why I hid them. No rhyme or reason. Never hid them before. Perhaps, after you came, I suddenly realised how very precious they were. And no one would dream of looking in a bread bin, now, would they – unless they wanted a sandwich?"

Charlie smiled. "I've got something to show you," he said. He put his hand in his pocket and passed its contents to the old lady.

She closed her hand then opened it and stared at what lay there.

"A penknife. A rather nice one with a horn handle. Where did you get it? What does this mean, Charlie Pringle? Have you got a story to tell *me* now?"

"I found it in my pocket."

Then Charlie told her everything, about Billy and Alice and how he'd pulled her from the rubble and given her the wooden mouse – about the warden – and then about finding Stephen in the old factory.

"It's the strangest dream I've ever had," he said at last, watching her face.

She looked back at him, very hard.

"You're sure it was just a dream?"

"It must have been," said Charlie. "But it was so real, and my hands were dirty – and look, this is where I scraped my leg – and cut my hand."

"What about the penknife? Where did that come from then if it was only a dream?"

"I don't know. I must have picked it up somewhere. It doesn't make any sense."

Mrs Tyrer's eyebrows were raised. "It makes sense to me. Remember what I said about wrinkles in time – ripples on the water? So you gave the mouse back to Alice. Good. It was probably meant for her anyway. That's what he used the penknife for. I bet it was going to be her Christmas present."

Charlie shook his head in astonishment.

"Do you really think so?"

It was too fantastic. But it was beginning to make some kind of sense. He would have to give it some thought. "I don't know. It's really weird."

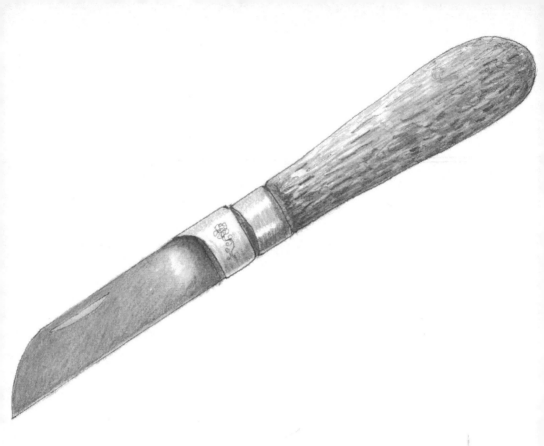

"But very exciting. So why didn't you come to see me on Friday night?"

"Don't you know? Mary-Lou was so ill. We thought ... Well, we didn't *really* think it, but we were so worried. She was rushed into hospital. She's still here but she is coming out tomorrow."

"Oh, I'm so sorry. And I'm glad she's better. Mary-Lou and little Alice. You can have a lovely Christmas now."

"What about you? What are you going to do? Will you go into a home?"

"I will not! Who told you such a thing?"

Charlie smiled. "Are you coming home then?"

"I pity anyone who tries to stop me. Remember the broomstick?"

"If someone picks you up, will you come into school one day and tell everyone about Guy and the Victoria Cross he won?"

"Yes, Charlie Pringle."

"And will you tell them all your other stories?"

"If I have enough breath. And will you tell them about Billy Porter and his friend, Charlie Pringle, how together they saved little Alice's life?"

"Billy Porter? How do you know his name?"

"Wait till I come home, Charlie Pringle, then I have something to show you."

Third on the list was Stephen. When Charlie arrived at the ward, he could see Mr and Mrs Cropper standing beside Stephen's bed. Stephen was dressed but his ankle was in a thick bandage. Mrs Cropper turned and saw him. Her red mouth smiled.

Mr Cropper, stiff in his dark suit, nodded.

Stephen just stared.

Charlie lifted a hand. "I'll see you tomorrow," he said, "when you come home." *Poor Stephen*, he kept thinking, *poor Stephen*.

****

A week later, Mrs Tyrer and Charlie were sitting at her table. The pot of tea was on the trivet and Charlie's mum had sent down some warm buttered scones.

"What a treat!" said Mrs Tyrer, tucking into one of them. "Eeh, but it's good to be home."

She opened an old exercise book with a crinkly red cover and marks on it like the tea stains of a century. "My mother's diary," she said. "Or at least, one of them. She really did put the strangest things in her diaries. Recipes, poems cut out of magazines, food bills, lists of all the jam she made – and interesting snippets out of newspapers." She unfolded a long strip of yellowing newspaper.

It was dated 10th November, 1932.

Charlie read the headline. 'Amy Johnson, the World's Greatest Airwoman,' and there was a picture of a woman with goggles and an old-fashioned flying helmet.

"Now there's a real hero, or should I say heroine. She wasn't much older than me." Then she gave him a tiny square which explained how to get your Christmas rations in 1940, and that children were allowed 8 oz. of chocolate. Before he could read any more, Mrs Tyrer opened three more pieces of newspaper. January 6th 1942, January 13th 1942, January 10th 1942. They were pictures of London, Sheffield and Swansea after the Blitz.

Charlie's stomach lurched when he saw them. He remembered the dust and the smell and the eerie silence when the planes had gone. He looked at Mrs Tyrer. Was this the important something she had wanted to show him?

She was watching his face, a mischievous gleam in her eye, knowing what he was thinking. She gave him a picture of a rowing boat, low in the water. It was the 'Noah's Ark', just as she had described it, with the cockerel sitting on Joe's head. Charlie laughed. The caption read, 'Noah's Ark comes safely to dry land'.

Then, "Are you ready?" she said.

Charlie nodded, not sure what he had to be ready for. Mrs Tyrer handed him another tiny snippet. On the top of it, were the words, 'Mystery of Blitz Hero'. And this is what Charlie read.

'A mystery boy has been credited with rescuing eighteen-month-old, Alice Porter, from the ruin of the house where she lived with her mother and brother, Billy. The house in Valmont Street was flattened to the ground in last night's bombing and rescuers say it was a miracle anyone got out alive. Sadly, however, young Billy Porter, eleven, was killed. The mystery boy disappeared while attention was given to the search for Billy. But that is not the end of it. Earlier, Warden Walter Tuffnell accosted a boy running through the streets without his gas mask. When questioned, the boy gave his name as Charlie Pringle and said he came from Priory Street, but no one of that name is known there. According to Mrs Porter, he deserves a medal and she is anxious to trace him. If anyone knows of his whereabouts ...'

"Have a cup of tea," said Mrs Tyrer. "You've gone a bit pale."

"I can't remember what I did with the gas mask," said Charlie. "I must have dropped it in the rubble."

"It wasn't a dream then?"

He shook his head slowly.

"I knew he was there for a reason," she said. "What a story you can write now."

"But no one will believe it. How can they? I'm not sure I do."

"You've got the newspaper to prove it."

"They'll say it's just a coincidence."

"And that you've got a wonderful imagination. And they'd be right. Adventures like that only happen to people with wonderful imaginations."

She opened another piece of paper, but this was not newspaper. It was the copy of an official report about Flight-Lieutenant Guy Wilson who had been on patrol over Southampton in a Hurricane, and decided to chase a Junkers.

One glance was enough.

"I've read this before," said Charlie, excitedly.

"It's in a book."

Mrs Tyrer smiled. "Is it really? Goodness. Life is just full of coincidences. Everything fits together like a jigsaw puzzle."

"It's the story Stephen was going to use. He was pretending it was his Granddad. You're in the story too, aren't you? You're the Red Cross nurse he was engaged to. Why didn't you marry him?"

"One flight too many, my dear. He tried to get home, but couldn't make it. Crashed in a field in Lincolnshire. They found his plane and buried him in his hometown in Scotland. That's where I met him before the war."

"So you married Arthur?"

"Arthur and his seven-penny teapot. He was a good man."

"Can I still visit you, even though I've got enough stories?"

"I'd be hurt if you didn't. Anyway, I haven't told you about the spy on the train."

"Will you come in to school before Christmas to see our display?"

"Try and stop me. I'll hire a taxi."

Now that could have been the end of the story and the beginning of a friendship, but it isn't – the end I mean – not quite.

Mrs Tyrer talked about coincidences. Strange things, I'm sure you'll agree, and we're not done with them yet. Perhaps it was the magic of the moon drifting like a silk-sailed barge down Charlie's stretch of the canal, or perhaps it was, as Mrs Tyrer said, a wrinkle in time. Anyway, this is what happened after.

Mrs Tyrer came into school in Charlie's dad's old Ford Fiesta. She was treated like a celebrity, given a bunch of flowers and a cup of tea. Then, in the middle of a chat to Mrs Taylor, and while she was looking at all the bits and pieces of the War displayed on the table and the walls, Mrs Tyrer gasped with surprise. There was her photo, the young nurse surrounded by injured soldiers, all of them smiling – and alongside it, another one. The same nurse standing with one young soldier in a wheel chair, his head heavily bandaged. She stared fixedly at it.

"Are you all right?" asked Mrs Taylor.

"That's Dawson, Private Peter Dawson. Terrible head injuries. Came in that second night from Dunkirk. Such a mess he was in, never thought he'd live. But that's not my photo. Where did it come from?"

"It's Wesley's great-granddad," said Charlie from behind her.

"Good gracious me! Is he ...?"

"Yes, I am still alive, and kicking. Though I do have a few scars and a limp. Hello Nurse Hughes. Good to see you again after all these years."

115

Then Mrs Tyrer simply had to sit down. When she had almost recovered and Wesley's great-granddad had promised to visit her and chat about old times, Charlie delivered the last surprise.

"Open your hand, Mrs Tyrer," he said.

She did as she was told, and Charlie placed something small and wooden in it.

When she looked, Mrs Tyrer could hardly believe her eyes. It was the wooden mouse.

"Full circle," she said. "Who has it now?"

"Millie Spencer's grandma. Her name's Alice and she kept it because her brother Billy made it for her when she was a baby, before he died in the Blitz."

What could she say? What could anyone say – except, "I could do with another cup of tea."

Dreams and heroes – that's what it was all about – and love that can reach through time.

"Mum wants to know if you'll spend Christmas with us, Mrs Tyrer."

"Only if the lift's working," she said, smiling.

"Dad said he'll carry you if it isn't – even though he's got a bad back."

"Then I'd love to, Charlie Pringle. Thank you."

"I'm making you a present. It's not as good as your Auntie Jinnie's box, but it's full of surprises."

"Just like you, Charlie Pringle," said Mrs Tyrer, "just like you."

Post Script

I suppose there is still one tiny loose end. Charlie's mountain bike. You're wondering if he ever got it. Well, six months after her ninety-first birthday, old Mrs Tyrer died peacefully in her sleep. She left a little something to a distant niece and nephew, who were so busy with their own lives, they almost never came to see her. The rest of her savings and all her belongings, including the Victoria Cross, she left to her friend Charlie with instructions that he was to buy something nice for everyone and spend the rest on a holiday. So Charlie and his dad bought three bikes and a seat for Mary-Lou, and they all went to the Lake District for a fortnight. Plenty of mountains there. Plenty of streams – and buzzards – and water gurgling up from the ground. Plenty of ducks too, for Mary-Lou.

****

I am grateful to my aunt, Edith May Langley, for sharing with me memories of her early life and her experiences during the war. She is, in essence, Mrs Tyrer. Apart from the Victoria Cross episode her stories are true and I still have the carnation and the newspaper account of the boat rescue. In an unremarkable life, tiny, remarkable things can happen and I wish she had lived to see how her own stories and memories became an important part of this book.